She swept a protective hand over her abdomen.

Very few people would have been able to guess that she was pregnant at this moment. Would the father of her child have been one of them?

"Erin, if he finds out..." Maria shuddered at the thought, unable to even finish the sentence. "I just need some time. And then, when I'm ready, I'll tell Micha."

"Tell me what, *cara*?"

Maria spun round in shock, coming face-to-face with Micha.

"I saw you leave," she whispered in horror.

"Well, I came back," he said, grim-faced and hard-eyed. "And now I think it's time that you tell me exactly what's going on, whether you're ready or not."

His gaze bored into hers, flicked down to where her hand was on her abdomen and rose back up to her face, eyes widening, lips parting in shock.

"You're pregnant."

A brand-new and captivating trilogy from Harlequin Presents author Pippa Roscoe.

Filthy Rich Italians

One billionaire family...three convenient proposals!

Powerful heirs Antonio, Enzo and Maria have found themselves in a bind. Their cunning grandfather has been scheming behind the scenes to ensure that his billion-euro company stays in the family—whether they like it or not! Wedding bells are certainly ringing— but do they signify business deals, or could there be more than money at stake...?

Six years ago, strangers Antonio and Ivy entered into a convenient marriage. Now, to save his family company, Antonio needs a divorce—but the judge won't grant it! The couple must prove that they've tried everything to make their marriage work, but after two weeks together in Tuscany, will a separation still be a straightforward solution...?

Inconveniently Wed

Erin Carter will stop at nothing to buy back her family company. And the new owner is willing to sell, on one condition: She has to marry his billionaire playboy grandson! But Enzo Rossetti will not be anyone's pawn. So when he overhears a beautiful stranger's plan to trap him into marriage, he decides to play her at her own game...

The Rossetti Ring Requirement

Maria Gallo is furious to find Micha Rufina, wrongful CEO of *her* family company and the man who broke her heart, on her doorstep. Micha needs his rival's help to run the company. But she's got her own bombshell to drop— she's pregnant with his child! And now Micha won't settle for anything less than marriage...

Their Boardroom Baby

All available now!

THEIR BOARDROOM BABY

PIPPA ROSCOE

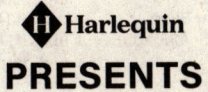

PRESENTS

If you purchased this book without a cover you should be aware that this book is stolen property. It was reported as "unsold and destroyed" to the publisher, and neither the author nor the publisher has received any payment for this "stripped book."

ISBN-13: 978-1-335-21352-5

Their Boardroom Baby

Copyright © 2026 by Pippa Roscoe

All rights reserved. No part of this book may be used or reproduced in any manner whatsoever without written permission.

Without limiting the exclusive rights of any author, contributor or the publisher of this publication, any unauthorized use of this publication to train generative artificial intelligence (AI) technologies is expressly prohibited. Harlequin also exercises their rights under Article 4(3) of the Digital Single Market Directive 2019/790 and expressly reserves this publication from the text and data mining exception.

This is a work of fiction. Names, characters, places and incidents are either the product of the author's imagination or are used fictitiously. Any resemblance to actual persons, living or dead, businesses, companies, events or locales is entirely coincidental.

For questions and comments about the quality of this book, please contact us at CustomerService@Harlequin.com.

TM and ® are trademarks of Harlequin Enterprises ULC.

 Harlequin Enterprises ULC
22 Adelaide St. West, 41st Floor
Toronto, Ontario M5H 4E3, Canada
www.Harlequin.com

HarperCollins Publishers
Macken House, 39/40 Mayor Street Upper,
Dublin 1, D01 C9W8, Ireland
www.HarperCollins.com

Printed in Lithuania

Pippa Roscoe lives in Norfolk near her family and makes daily promises to herself that this is the day she'll leave the computer to take a long walk in the countryside. She can't remember a time when she wasn't dreaming about handsome heroes and innocent heroines. Totally her mother's fault, of course—she gave Pippa her first romance to read at the age of seven! She is inconceivably happy that she gets to share those daydreams with you all. Follow her on X @pipparoscoe.

Books by Pippa Roscoe

Harlequin Presents

The Wife the Spaniard Never Forgot
His Jet-Set Nights with the Innocent
In Bed with Her Billionaire Bodyguard
Twin Consequences of That Night
Forbidden Until Midnight

A Billion-Dollar Revenge

Expecting Her Enemy's Heir

The Greek Groom Swap

Greek's Temporary "I Do"

Filthy Rich Italians

Inconveniently Wed
The Rossetti Ring Requirement

Visit the Author Profile page at Harlequin.com for more titles.

PROLOGUE

He had to find Maria. He... Micha could barely pull his thoughts together. They'd scattered like the marbles he'd seen other children play with on the streets. He couldn't... He didn't...

Gio Gallo, the man he'd had the temerity—and desperation—to try and steal from, the man who had plucked Micha and his mother from the streets, given him a job, an education, a place to live, a future, the man to whom he owed *everything*, had just broken his heart.

Ask her. Ask her and see what she says.

Micha was a few days from his eighteenth birthday. And he'd been happy. He'd been pinch-me-hard-because-this-didn't-happen-to-people-like-me happy. Gio had been his fairy godfather far beyond the time when Micha had believed in fairytales—if he ever had.

He'd grown up hard and quick, forced to do and see things most adults never did. Not that he'd ever lay the blame at his mother's feet. She'd done the best she could. She'd done *whatever* she could and he forced his thoughts away from the darkness that filled his mind when memories of the past came calling. His father had run off before he was born, leaving his mother saddled with debts she had no hope of paying, and debtors who had plenty of ideas. He'd been on edge, hovering between desperation and hopelessness when he'd run across Gio.

Gio, who had given him everything.

Gio, who wanted to send him away.

Gio had brought him into his business, his family and his sprawling family estate in Tuscany, and Micha had thrived. As for the rest of his family? They were not all like Gio, who had seen in him what no money could have bought—an intelligence that matched his own and a determination that would achieve great things, given half the chance. No, instead, most of the Gallos simply saw a half Italian and half Russian illegitimate street urchin who would never amount to anything.

Maria hadn't thought that though. She and Antonio had never treated him as anything but an equal. They had befriended him, and they became inseparable. The Three Musketeers, that's what they had been called. He hadn't understood the reference at first and had to look it up, but he liked it. Three friends who would do anything for each other.

Ask her and see what she says.

Micha had genuinely thought he and Maria had been careful enough that no one had known about their relationship. He stumbled over the word *love*. He felt it, but could still hardly believe that someone like Maria could feel that way for him. But he *adored* her. She filled his every thought. She made his heart ache just at the sight of her.

But Gio wanted to send him away.

Micha had always wanted to work for Gio. He'd wanted to repay the man who had changed his and his mother's entire lives. He was going to work for Gio and so was

Maria. Because Maria wanted to run Gallo Group—the international conglomerate that Gio ruled with an iron fist.

But the only way that Gio would allow that to happen was if she married Antonio—her adopted cousin. Gio Gallo was *fixated* on the union of his two grandchildren, having given up fully on his own, useless children.

Micha had thought that if he could just prove himself, if he could show the old man just how good he was, Gio might eventually change his mind. He'd thought he would have time.

'I'm sending you to Paris,' Gio had announced that morning.

'That's…kind of you, Mr Gallo, but I'd rather stay here. To be near—' *Maria* '—my mother.' The guilt at the lie twisted in his soul.

'This is no problem. I will be providing you both with accommodation.'

'I have—' *friends* '—colleagues here. And I was just beginning to grow—'

From behind his desk, Gio had pulled up to his full height, the black-eyed glare stopping Micha's words so much so that he nearly bit his tongue.

'It's just that—' Micha had tried again.

'No,' Gio said. The word a bullet. 'It's not your mother, it's not your friends or your career prospects. What it *is*,' he said, stressing the word, 'is an impossibility.'

'Sir, I—'

'She is not meant for you,' Gio spat, the poison dropping into Micha's skin. 'You know my feelings on this.'

Micha clenched his jaw.

'But, really, it's not *my* feelings you have to worry

about. You know how much she wants to lead this company. At seventeen, she already has a better business head than my children do at twice her age. She was born for this. She wants this. And she *will* choose this over you, Micha.'

Micha huffed out a disbelieving breath.

She wouldn't.

'Ask her, Micha. Ask her and see what she says.'

He couldn't say it was sadness that he'd seen in the old man's eyes. Pity and such things were far beyond Gio's emotional capabilities. But it didn't matter, Micha thought to himself. She would choose him.

Micha found her lounging on the large verdant lawn of Gio's Tuscan villa laughing with Antonio and for a moment a vicious splinter of jealousy cut through his heart. They *did* look good together. Together they could run Gallo Group and life would be easy and rich and...

'Micha!' Maria called when she caught sight of him, her gaze happy and her face bright.

His heart shuddered and he forced a smile to his lips.

'*Ciao bella*,' Micha called as he drew closer.

Antonio raised a hand to clap him on the back when he arrived.

'Good, take this one off my hands, please. She's driving me round the bend. I have to go, Mama is waiting,' he said easily, dropping a kiss to Maria's cheek and another slap to Micha's back. 'Look after her,' Antonio called as he loped back up to the estate.

Maria smiled up at him and patted the ground beside her, Micha dropping to his knees strangely out of breath.

'I have to ask you something,' he said, focusing on the tumble of dark curls that surrounded her like a halo.

'Hello, how are you? Well, thank you, and you?' Maria said on a laugh which petered out when she saw the look on his face. 'Of course, you can ask me whatever you like,' she said, placing a hand on his forearm.

'What would…?' Micha swallowed.

Tell her.

No.

Tell her why you're asking.

'What would you do to become head of this company? If Gio offered it to you? What would you do?' The words rushed out of Micha's mouth, his heart thudding painfully, as if already he was running from her answer, as if already he was rushing to pack his bags for Paris.

Would you do it? Would you marry Antonio if Gio asked?

Maria blinked at him, pulling a strand of her curls that the wind had blown across her face. Her smile bright and her eyes gleaming.

'Anything,' she said, enthusiastically. 'Anything. You know that.'

And then she leaned forward and pressed a kiss against his lips, not knowing that her declaration had broken him forever.

CHAPTER ONE

Eleven years later...

THE SOUND OF her heels against the marble flooring of the foyer of Gallo Group headquarters in France made Maria Aurora Guilia Gallo feel like a *boss*. The boss that she would be within *months*.

Some may have found it petty that she had taken the Gallo Group jet from Italy to France for the sole purpose of rubbing that very fact into Micha Rufina's face, but she didn't care.

The receptionist looked at her warily and Maria realised that it was a very real possibility that she had just growled. Out loud.

She shook it off, sending a ripple across the billowing cream silk button-up shirt, tucked into the camel-coloured cashmere trousers pressed to perfection with a flawless crease down the centre of each leg. The patent leather cream one-of-a-kind Louboutins—the ones clicking *so* satisfyingly towards the private elevator that only family and board members had access to—were her favourite pair.

Every single item of clothing, down to the lace basque, had been intentionally chosen. They were pieces of her armour. The armour she would wear to the final battle she ever had with Micha Rufina—her nemesis. Her enemy. And if he had been anything before that, anything more, she had forced herself to burn it from her memory until all that remained was a jagged scar, hidden so deep, her heart could barely remember it.

She arrived at the lift, swiped her key card and waited.

A woman came hurrying up to her.

'Mademoiselle Gallo, it's so lovely...' she trailed off when Maria cut her a glare. 'Does Mr Rufina know you're here?' The pitch of the poor woman's voice rose into the stratosphere.

'No,' Maria replied, turning back to the lift, ending any and all hopes of further conversation the receptionist may have had.

To her right was the bank of public lifts that would take the building's staff to whatever floor they worked on. She was aware of a few of the staff casting surreptitious glances her way as they left for the evening. Or trying to at least.

At first, Maria had bemoaned the way that she drew the male gaze.

'They'll never take me seriously,' she'd complained to her cousin Antonio. 'All they see is this,' she'd said, yanking on the thick tumble of long black curls. 'And these,' she'd said, pushing out her chest. Antonio had barked out a laugh and pushed her out of his face, telling her to 'get those things away from me.' They'd both ended up crying with laughter. 'Then, *mi amor*,' he'd said, 'make them take you seriously in spite of it.'

He'd been right. As always. Her cousin, her favourite family member in the whole wide world, and not just because the rest of them were worse than a den of poisonous vipers out for whatever cent they could get their greedy little hands on. No, Antonio had always been there supporting her, cheering her on, even when her own parents wouldn't. And so what if, for the last six years, Antonio had been a little distracted by his company, and avoiding the wrath of their grandfather. He was *still* the only person she could rely on to help her.

And so—despite having worked for longer, and harder, than most of the family members there—she had always used her clothing with near deadly intent.

Dress the part, act the part, get the part.

And today she had dressed *rich*. *Expensive*. She had dressed with the kind of class that went beyond money. And she'd done it for one reason and one reason only. She wanted Micha to know that she was so far beyond his reach they may as well be on different planets.

She wanted the boy she'd all but grown up with to know that this was the last time he would ever see her, no matter what he'd meant to her grandfather. The grandfather she had looked up to, had loved with everything she had in her, but who had never once seen her as worthy. The grandfather who had been a complex, deeply difficult man, but who sometimes she'd thought she understood. Until he had passed away and his last will and testament had been read. The shock waves that had rippled out had been catastrophic for some, but for her and Antonio? Life changing.

Because Gio's last will and testament revealed that no matter what they had done in the last six years—Antonio marrying someone else, Maria working every hour god sent to prove her worth—Gio Gallo had never given up on his eccentric and utterly irrational plan for her and Antonio to marry and together produce the perfect heir to inherit and run his empire.

It didn't matter that they were already Gallos. Antonio was adopted and she was female, these two things marring them in some way for their grandfather. But a child from the two of them? *That* was what Gio had wanted from the beginning. And if they didn't marry and fulfil the terms of the will? The entire company would be handed over to Micha Rufina—something Maria would *never* allow to happen while she still had breath in her lungs.

Antonio felt the same, which was why he had agreed to marry her in name only, to fulfil the terms of the will. Once Antonio got a divorce from the woman he'd married for convenience six years ago, he would then be free to marry *her*. And once they were married, once they had inherited the company, he would sign over his share of the company that he had absolutely no interest in and they would go their separate ways. Him to his business, Alessina International, and her to Gallo Group. And no one would ever look down on her again.

Ding.

The elevator doors opened and she entered a small cubicle big enough for three people at a push. The rose gold mirrored glass threw her image back at her in soft reflections and she counted the floors down as she rose higher up the building, all the way to the penthouse.

She had been to the Paris office of Gallo Group several times over the past six years, but made sure to do so when Micha wasn't there. She, unlike many others, had *not* been surprised by the meteoric rise of the boy Gio had taken under his wing all those years ago. No, she knew something of Micha's mettle.

And it was cold, hard and impenetrable.

But still, even she had to begrudgingly respect the man's business acumen. And where others in the family had snidely remarked about the 'transferable skills' of begging and thieving on the streets of Roma, she had only seen survival and determination, her sympathy for the boy she had once known refusing to budge on that instance. But she had also learned at her cost not to underestimate him.

Maria arrived at the penthouse floor with a ding and the lift doors parted to an exquisite reception area, continuing the use of the Gallo Group's brand colours of rose gold and cream, she saw with no small sense of satisfaction.

She had been integral to the rebranding three years before and while the board had raised objections Gio had seen the sense in her plan. Gallo Group's global perception skewed towards older males and while that had worked in the past, women were the future. And it was time for the Gallos to damn well catch up.

Frowning when she realised that the receptionist was not at her desk, she checked her watch. It was, she realised, after six in the evening, but it was strange that Micha's secretary would have left already.

She made her way on thickly piled carpet towards the regional CEO's office. The doors were wide open and unable to help herself, she entered and—just like the previous times she'd been here—immediately gravitated over to the window that stretched from floor to ceiling across one entire side of the huge office.

Many others might have boasted three-hundred-and-sixty-degree views. But what did that matter, when the one window of this office showed the Eiffel Tower in its entirety? Even as a little girl, she'd loved Paris. And her heart sighed just to see the most famed image of France stretched out before her.

For a moment, she wondered what it would have been like to be here under different circumstances, but before that half-formed fantasy could even take hold, she felt the hairs on the back of her neck raise.

'What are you doing here, *cara*?'

'You don't get to call me that,' she said, her words filled with the poison she wished she could use to hurt him the way that he'd hurt her.

Micha saw her flinch at his words, at how the muscles tightened all the way across her shoulders and back. He clenched his jaw, instantly regretting the word that had slipped past his usually ruthless self-control.

'How did you get in here?' he demanded, raising the armour that had broken at her shocking and surprising appearance in his office. He stalked over to his desk to put down the folder he had in his hands. And to buy himself some time to get over the impact of the sudden and perturbing sight of Maria Gallo.

He had seen her only a few weeks before at Alessina Gallo's party. Antonio's mother was trying her best to keep the disparate threads of the family together in her father's absence. The man's will had left more than the company without leadership, and both the family and the business were at risk of breaking apart because of it.

'I walked.'

'Oh really? I thought you might have flown in on your broomstick,' he muttered under his breath.

'How original, Micha. Calling me a witch.'

Maria's words lashed across his skin and he winced. He knew how often she was belittled by family members who were half outraged that she dared to be more than just a pretty face. And while she and he had a somewhat fractious—okay, downright toxic—relationship, he was nothing like those who called her names like the one he had just used.

'You know I meant it differently,' he growled.

And her lack of response told him that she *did* know it. Otherwise, she would have nailed his balls to the wall.

'Where is your secretary?' she asked and he looked up to find her standing behind the chair opposite his desk, her hands gripping onto the back.

'Why? Afraid to be alone with me?' he couldn't help but taunt.

'From what I remember, there is little to be afraid of,' she bit back.

Ouch. How could he have forgotten that her tongue was quick and that her wit was harsh?

He locked his jaw before he could say anything that would take them further down a road neither of them wanted to travel. Frankly he didn't have time for this, for *her*. While the rest of the Gallos were playing games he seemed to be the only person with sense trying to keep the ship afloat, rather than deciding—or caring—who steered her.

'She's at a training seminar,' he said, lying about his secretary's whereabouts. The poor woman had been driven to the edge by the hounding the various outliers of the

Gallo family were giving her, so he had let her go home early. Not everyone was privy to the contents of the will and it was causing problems.

Not that Maria would have cared about that. Oh no. All she probably cared about was that she would finally get her hands on the company that she—in all honesty—deserved. And if she did? She'd probably sack him. Perhaps that's why she was here. Perhaps—

That pulled him up short.

So much so that she caught him staring at her.

'What?' she asked.

Micha shook his head, not willing to put the idea in her head if it wasn't already. Which he doubted. He cursed under his breath.

'Out with it, Maria. I have things to do. Contracts to secure.'

She laughed, as if it were genuinely amusing to her that he actually worked here. He wanted to pinch the bridge of his nose, but that would give away his frustration. And it pleased him no end that it was her inability to ruffle him that caused her the greatest irritation.

'Sure. Why not. The last act of a drowning man. Have at it, Rufina.'

He nodded, shooing her away with his hand, until he realised the subtext beneath her words.

Last act.

Why not.

Cristo, she was going to do it. She was going to marry Antonio to get her hands on the company.

His hands, fists, pressed into the table, concealing the white knuckles betraying his feelings, and for one single heartbeat—nothing but blind fury, masked, leashed and utterly denied by the next pump of blood around his body.

Slowly, he raised his gaze to hers, inch by inch, covering the cream shirt and trousers she wore, luxurious, rich, expensive. The pearls at her neck, the free-falling thick curls that dropped over one shoulder. She'd probably dressed just to remind him that he'd once been nothing more than a street urchin, while she'd always been an heiress.

By the time he'd reached her face, her expression told him that his guess had been true. The gleam of satisfaction shone like a north star that would never point to a home for him. He thought…*minchia!* He didn't know what he thought.

Unlike the rest of the family, who had never even heard of Ivy McKellen, Micha knew all about the convenient marriage that took place six years ago between Ivy and Antonio, meant solely to circumvent the pressure piled on by Gio Gallo for Antonio to marry Maria. But their relationship was a lot more complicated than Maria knew.

Micha had met Ivy. He'd seen the grit and determination that drove her, even in her darkest hours. And more than that, Micha had liked her. Whether Antonio knew it or not, Ivy was a near perfect match for him and *Cristo*, if he had even an ounce of intellect, he wouldn't let her slip away. Certainly not for the sake of a damn company—no matter how many billions it was worth.

And it was most definitely worth billions.

'What have you done, *cara*?' he demanded, his voice low to his own ears with a warning that he knew she wouldn't heed.

'What I had to do,' she shot back just as hard and just as low, and damn it if it didn't turn him on.

As a girl, she'd been all soft curves and sighs, giggles and curiosity. As a woman? She would be something else altogether. For a moment, the apocryphal sight of her entwined in Antonio's embrace rose in his mind, making him nearly want to retch.

'Antonio and I will be married by the end of the month,' she declared.

He barked out a laugh. 'That's ridiculous. He doesn't love you like that.'

'Who said anything about love?'

'*Dio mio*, are you so desperate for this company that marriage means nothing to you?' he accused. 'Vows before god, your family, your *mother*?'

Maria felt her cheeks heat with anger and her pulse pick up beneath her skin.

'My mother?' Maria scoffed. How dare he talk about her mother? About marriage. About *vows*. 'I'm surprised you managed to say all that with a straight face, Micha. Or is this just another little ploy to shame me, to manipulate me, *distract me*? "Look over here, Maria," all the while, you're over there…playing another game entirely.'

Bitterness dripped like poison between them.

'Well, I won't fall for it. Not this time,' she said, ignoring the way dark red slashes appeared on cheekbones she'd known both women *and* men to swoon over. 'My marriage to Antonio *will* happen,' she insisted. 'The company *will* be mine. And you *will* be gone.'

Micha's only response was the slight narrowing of his eyes.

Oh, damn this man! She was trying to have an epic, victorious moment and he wasn't doing what she'd spent years, a near decade, imagining. He was supposed to be on his knees, begging for mercy.

She turned away from him, wanting to hide her reaction to his words. He knew. He *knew* what her parents' marriage had been like. How distant and cold, and unbearable it had been for her. The endless sniping and degrading, demeaning and belittling from her father—the near horrific silence of her mother. She'd once begged and pleaded with them to get a divorce, hoping that perhaps then she might be able to find space to breathe from the suffocation she had grown up with. And ironically, it had been the one single thing in their entire marriage that they agreed on.

There would be no divorce.

Throughout her childhood she had sought sanctuary with Antonio and, yes, even at one point, Micha. At many points even—but she refused to dwell on those times. Together the three of them had run amok throughout Tuscany and it had felt as if the entire world was at their feet. They had been the only family her age or near enough— distant cousins removed more than once were either older or not yet born. As for siblings, for her father, her mother's inability to bear a second child only furthered the distance between the wife who had failed him and the daughter who would always be a disappointment instead of the heir apparent he'd always wanted.

Antonio and Micha had been her salvation. They had protected her, distracted her. Antonio's mother had called them the Three Musketeers, and they had imagined playing with swords, attacking their enemies and cutting down their foes.

Well, she was still doing that. Only now, her weapon of choice was marriage. Marriage to Antonio. Not marriage to the boy she had once given her sovery-precious heart to. She braced herself before turning back to where Micha was riffling through some pages on his desk, still standing.

And oddly, she knew that he would stand for as long as she did. Something gentlemanly that he had inherited from her grandfather. He might not have been related to her by blood, but Micha carried some things from Gio Gallo that were instinctive. The way he held himself. His manners. It was perhaps a goddamn relief that he hadn't inherited the man's morals. Micha was ruthless enough by himself. He didn't need that in his blood too.

'It will, perhaps, be a little harder than you think to get rid of me,' he said, without bothering to look at her. It made her feel small. It made her feel dismissed. But she was done allowing Micha Rufina to make her feel those things. She'd had enough of that when she was sixteen.

'On the contrary. I think you'll find it quite expeditiously done with two little words. You're fired.'

'You underestimate how much I do for this company, Maria.'

'And you overestimate how much I care,' she shot back, recklessly. Because no matter what had passed between them, no matter where in the world they were, he had *always* made her reckless.

'You'd do it, wouldn't you? You'd fire me, and damn the consequences?' he asked, a strange light in his eye.

'Absolutely.'

'No questions?'

'None.'

'I have one,' he said, surprising her a little.

'Shoot.'

'Do you really believe that you hate me?'

She stilled, sensing the danger in his question.

'Your arrogance is truly exceptional, Micha,' she fired back.

'Answer the question.'

'Believe? I don't *believe*. I *know* how much I hate you, Micha. Much as that might shock you. If the rumours are true, you've built quite the dance card from the women here in Paris.'

'Careful, Maria. Sounds a little like jealousy to me.'

Maria scoffed. 'It's not jealousy, Micha,' she said sweeping her gaze over him, 'it's disgust.'

He threw his head back and barked a laugh, dismissing her put-down. The long column of his neck was stubbled with the shadow of a beard she knew he'd shaved that morning.

Dressed in a three-piece suit, he should have looked all business and boring. But damn it, he looked anything but. The grey superfine wool of the suit was cut to fit him perfectly, with a white shirt made from Egyptian cotton. He filled it all out to perfection.

'See, I don't think that you hate me,' he said circling back round to his earlier question, his tongue sweeping out for barely a second before his teeth plunged into his bottom lip, as he looked at her in a very dominant and utterly unbusinesslike way.

No. This? Here? Right now? He was pure alpha male. A predator stalking its prey.

And she was the prey.

He shrugged off his suit jacket and hung it on the back of his chair, before coming around from behind the large ornate table that had once been used by her grandfather. He came to stand in front of her as he unhooked his cufflinks and pocketed them, before rolling back the sleeves of his shirt, something she found inexplicably fascinating.

He leaned back against the desk, arms folded across his chest—pulling the shirt tight across his chest and biceps beneath the matching grey waistcoat—his gaze running up and down the length of her body insolently, *carelessly*, heating every single place it touched.

And he knew it too.

Micha took his time, and his fill. Oh, he was aware how crass it was, but at this point he realised that he had very little to lose.

For years, he'd behaved himself. He'd done as Gio wanted, confined himself to the little box that Gio Gallo had put him in, safely away from the proximity of his favourite *female* grandchild. The gender qualifier wasn't important to him, but it had been to Gio. Gio, who had all but been near maniacal about who his business empire went to after his death.

Gio had been obsessed with it going to a male of the family—but Antonio wasn't a Gallo by blood, his adoption by Alessina apparently not enough to satisfy the old man. But a marriage between Antonio and Maria—an adopted grandchild and a female grandchild?—that had seemed just about enough in Gio Gallo's mind.

And Micha? Oh, he'd been used as the stick to beat or threaten the Gallos with for years and Gio's death had not changed that. Micha would inherit the entire company, lock, stock and barrel, if Antonio and Maria didn't marry.

No one, not even the two people he'd once considered friends, *more* even, had ever once thought that he might actually be good at what he did here. That he might actually have added to the wealth of the Gallos—heaven forbid, that he might actually even deserve it. But then...not even Gio Gallo had truly thought that of Micha.

'I *do* hate you,' she ground out from between perfect white teeth, bared at him in a silent growl. 'And this? This is the last time you'll ever see me,' she announced with a flourish.

He smirked, unable to help himself.

'What's so funny?' she demanded, furious that her threat hadn't been met with trembling knees and chattering teeth.

She must have forgotten that he was built differently than the simpering, pathetic members of the Gallo clan on whom her ire would have worked.

'You. Threatening me.'

'It's not a threat, it's a promise.'

'Mmm,' he said, closing the distance between them in just a few short strides.

'What are you doing?' she asked, backing up, startled when her legs hit the back of the chair behind her.

'Whatever I want,' he replied, unable to take his gaze from her. His eyes searched, scored, imprinted every single moment of her onto his soul. The way that the silk of her shirt shivered when she breathed, the superbly fitting palazzo trousers, pressing against skin and curves he'd never once forgotten.

Oh, they'd not done much as teenagers, no matter

what Gio Gallo had thought. No matter what anyone had thought. Heavy petting, the Americans might have called it. But it hadn't mattered. He'd know her in one hundred years. Blind, deaf and unable to speak, he'd *know* her.

But she'd never really known him, had she?

'Stop it,' she said, trying to back up again.

'Why?' he asked, cocking his head to one side. 'What are you going to do? Fire me?' he taunted.

He pressed closer to her, knowing that he was invading her space, obsessively hunting the flush that started from the sliver of skin he could see in the V of her shirt and crept up her throat. The pulse that flickered at the base of her jaw. The tremble to her lips she tried to stop by pinning one beneath her teeth.

'Maria,' he warned.

'Yes?'

'That is not helping.' His voice was a growl.

She clenched her teeth together.

'You can't do this,' she said, putting her hands on him. His heart thundered at the press of her palm over it, and he finally gave in to the need that was coursing through his veins. The one he had spent years hiding, denying, destroying.

He'd been fooled into thinking he had it under control. But he was wrong. So wrong.

Maria looked up at him with huge dark brown eyes, her hair cascading in tumbled curls down her back, her lips parted as if on a gasp.

'Then stop me,' he commanded.

He waited.

He waited for the hands on his chest to push him away in disgust, the way he'd imagined her doing time and time and time again in the deepest, darkest dreams of half-formed memories and damaged desires.

He waited for her to turn her head to the side, to snub him as she so often did in public, their hostilities as much a spectator sport for the families as not.

He waited for her to hiss and spit and curse his name, to damn him to hell and back.

But she didn't. She did none of those things. Instead, she seemed as enthralled to this madness as he was. Her gaze, licking at him like flames that would devour. Hot, harsh, *demanding*.

'Stop me,' he half begged, himself no longer sure whether this was madness or mistake.

Her lush lips parted, but nothing came out.

He'd given her warning. She was certainly bold enough to refuse him if she wanted.

He claimed her mouth, already half open beneath his, no timid greeting of soft gentle touches. This was a clash, powerful, brash, possessive and demanding, consuming to the point of insanity. It was like coming home and leaving home all at once. Something earthily familiar and completely unknowable. Déjà vu and *jamais vu*, together at the same time.

They both pulled back, shocked, confused, glaring accusations at each other, breaths heaving, lips tingling.

'You—'

Micha cut her off before she could ruin it and claimed her once more. His hands thrust into her hair, shaping her head with his fingers, and she groaned her pleasure into his mouth and sank against his chest in wanton abandonment.

Dio mio.

CHAPTER TWO

Maria was utterly lost. Completely and without question. She felt as if she was made up of pure sensual delight, every place she could feel, delicious, every pulse a throb so perfectly pleasurable, it was near inconceivable.

From just a kiss.

Per dio!

She indulged the moan of sheer want creeping up the back of her throat, her mouth opening just a little wider, which Micha took full advantage of. The thrust of his tongue carnal, sending thousands of little shivers across her skin until she trembled from the weight of them.

Her hands fisted in his shirt, pulling it taut across his chest. She wanted it gone. She wanted the barrier between their skin incinerated. With shaking fingers, she slipped the buttons of his waistcoat free, her hands stretching out beneath the silk lining, and not so gently scratching the sides of his torso through the cotton of his shirt.

The growl of pleasure against her lips only spurred her on.

Mirroring her hands, his palms moved from her head to her hips, dragging her against him, against the hard ridge of his arousal. The noise she made, primal, instinctive, spun out from her mouth into him, and he turned them, walking her backwards until her backside met the large office table.

He lifted her, effortlessly, up onto the table and pushed his way between her legs in a move that was both possessive and domineering at the same time.

Oh, why was it *this* man? Why him?

Why was it only Micha who had ever made her this way? This crazy, this aroused, this hedonistic, this wanton?

She closed her eyes, her head falling back as his lips traversed the column of her throat and across her collarbone. Delight fanned out in sparks across her skin, sinking into her blood, her bones, her soul.

If she thought he'd stop, if she thought he'd lift the shirt from the waist of her trousers, she'd been wrong. Instead, with a near ruthless efficiency, he simply hooked his finger around the front of her basque and pulled, exposing her breasts to his sight and her nipples to his tongue.

Wet heat pooled instantly between her thighs and where she would have pulled her legs closed, she instead clamped around Micha's hips, securing him in place, so that he could tease every single erogenous zone she knew of.

She leaned back to give him more access, his mouth closing over one nipple, over the silk of her shirt, his tongue leaving a damp stain on her breast, cooling to tease the taut flesh as he turned his attention to the other.

Until, he returned hungrily to her mouth. With one hand on her jaw, and the other swept around her backside, pulling her hard against him, she felt devoured. Completely and utterly. There was no escape and she wanted none. Pleasure and pressure were building in her, the restlessness frustrating as what she wanted ebbed and flowed from her reach.

'Maria.'

Her name, half plea, half promise, on his lips, in his voice…it was as if it had travelled back through the years, drenched from the depths of her memories. She opened her eyes, and saw him gazing back.

Him.

Micha.

The boy who had broken her heart.

She shouldn't be doing this. She couldn't. Not again.

She pulled back from his hold, and she saw the moment the shutters came down, cutting her off from the savage heat of the previous moment.

'This was a mistake,' she said, scrabbling for the broken shards of her armour and pulling them about her defensively.

'Don't do that,' he warned, with a thread of darkness she'd not heard before.

'Don't what?'

'Don't demean this,' he commanded.

'Why? You did,' she threw at him as she pushed past him with her shoulder.

Micha reached out and clasped her wrist, stopping her when she would have left, spinning her back to face him. He had been talking about their kiss, but she was talking about the past. Her fury sparked gold shards of lightning in the depths of her chestnut-coloured eyes. He'd always been fascinated by the colour, as if one wasn't enough for her, she needed as many as she could get: browns, golds, some flashes of something near green.

The rest of her family had brown eyes so dark they appeared nearly black. But Maria had inherited her eyes from her mother, who had married into the Gallos. And now, they displayed fury in multicoloured hues.

'I went where your grandfather sent me,' Micha ground out. He refused to think back to that day, that time, when she'd severed his heart, gleefully telling him that she'd do anything to run Gallo Group, knowing that Gio had wanted her to marry Antonio. *Cristo*, here she was, exactly eleven years later, ready to do just that. He'd made the right decision then to leave. To protect himself and his mother. Because no one else would.

'You could have said no to him,' she accused.

This time he did laugh out loud. 'Yes, *cara*. Because we all know that Gio would have taken no for an answer.'

'You *could* have. You might have been the only one able to do it out of all of us,' she said, and he wondered whether he saw hurt there in her gaze or whether he was just so desperate to see it that he was imagining it.

'What about you?' he returned. 'When did you ever say no to your grandfather?'

She was shaking her head, sending the tumble of her curls swaying across her shoulders, when he let go of her wrist. Her obtuse denial infuriated him.

'You deny it? Even now you're rushing to do his bidding,' Micha pointed out. 'You feel nothing more for Antonio than familial love, yet you are going to marry him just as Gio wanted.'

'I'm going to marry Antonio because I want the company,' Maria insisted.

'Why that company? Why not any other company in the entire world? You're an incredible businesswoman. Your reputation is stellar. You're respected, financially solvent. *Cristo*, if you wanted to sell your shares in Gallo Group you would have millions at your disposal.'

You'd be free, he thought internally, the words sounding like an accusation and a plea at the same time.

'I don't want another company. I want this one. I want the one that I should have inherited all along, without having to do some silly tap dance. I want the one that, had I been born a man, would have been mine without question. I want the one that I have worked for my entire professional life. I want,' she said, her breathing harsh with the fury of her sense of injustice, 'the company that I have helped grow, whose wealth I have helped increase. I want what I've earned, Micha. I've earned Gallo Group. Far more than Antonio, who hasn't worked in it since he was twenty-one. Far more than any of the uncles that have sat on the board and done nothing but voted with their wallets.'

'Far more than me?' Micha asked finally when she paused to take a breath.

Maria glared at him, unable to say anything back. Because out of everyone, he was the only other person who had held a candle to what she'd given to Gallo Group. The only other person who could stand at the helm without ruining it—no matter what her family might think of him.

'Or have you become like the rest of your family and decided that I am far from your equal?' he said, finally ready to face the truth.

If they were burning bridges, then so be it. He would burn them all.

'I am not like them,' she hotly denied.

'But you don't think we are equals, do you?'

'You aren't family, Micha.'

The punch of air that fell from his lips was the only sign of the way she had cut him off at his knees. He'd always thought it, but never really wanted to believe it. But she'd *never* thought he was good enough. He wasn't like Antonio, who'd had the good graces to get himself adopted. No, no matter what he did, how hard he worked, he'd never shake the stigma of his humble origins, or the depths of what he'd been driven to do for his mother, for himself.

He looked down at her, seeing Maria in a new light. Beautiful, but cruelly removed.

She might think herself better than him, but that didn't stop her wanting him. And it certainly didn't stop him wanting her.

'You might not like me, Maria. Or think me good enough. But you still desire me, don't you?' he bit out. 'That must *really* sting,' he said, satisfied by the sight of the flare in her gaze.

'I don't know what you're talking about,' she tried to dismiss.

But he wasn't letting her get away with it. Not this time. If she'd come to kick him out on his backside once she took over the company, then he was going to make her work for it. She was going to have to admit a few things and he wasn't going to let her go until she had.

'Oh really? That's not what those breathy little moans you were making in my ear only moments ago suggested,' he taunted in a cruel whisper.

He knew how much that would hurt. Because it hurt him too. To want her so much, to be driven to almost demented lengths by the memory of what had been, the knowledge of what could have been and the awareness of what never would be.

'Go on, tell me how much you hated my kiss,' he demanded, pressing into her personal space, forcing her back a step.

'I—' She searched his gaze, knowing and understanding morphing into frustration. She couldn't lie, but she wouldn't admit it either.

'Tell me, Maria, how much you hated the feel of my mouth on your breast,' he said, his gaze dropping to her mouth. 'My touch on your skin.'

'Micha—'

'Tell me,' he said dropping his lips to the shell of her ear, as she hit the wall of the office and had nowhere else to go, 'how you hated me so much you haven't fantasised about this for *years*.'

Her breath poured in and out of her, raising her chest to his again and again, the flush on her cheeks, the pink of her lips so recently kissed, a warning, a flare.

'I...' She swallowed, her head leaning up to look at him, her eyes glowing and her skin flushed. 'I can't.'

'Because you *didn't* hate it?' he pushed. 'Because you *have* fantasised about this? Because...' He swallowed, daring her, daring himself to go as far as this would take them. 'Because you *do* want this?'

She nodded her head slowly, not once taking her eyes off him. As if she were as bound to this madness as he was. And in that moment, he wasn't sure who had just won the battle, because it might have required his own surrender.

Maria stared at the man who had just bared her deepest secret to the light of day. That no matter how much she hated him, for leaving her, for walking away as if she were nothing, as if what they had shared was nothing, she still wanted him. Needed him like an addiction that wouldn't quit.

'Yes,' she said, the confession wrenched from her lips. 'Are you happy now?' she demanded, breath heaving in her chest, lust clashing with injustice, with the near ache of misery.

But when she looked into his eyes, the rich swirls of a bitter chocolate that had once danced with laughter—so long ago she thought she might have made it up—she didn't see happiness. She didn't see victory. She saw the same frustrated need that she felt.

'Not at all, *cara*,' he said, finally answering her question.

Frantic energy sparked and hissed in the air between them as they edged closer and closer to a line that had been drawn between them years before. As if they both knew that once they crossed it, there would be no going back. And there would be no going forward either.

But she couldn't take it any more. She couldn't live like this—in this half-life, stuck in the middle of what had been and what could never be.

'You understand? What you're doing?' she asked, lips trembling, from desire or fear she didn't know. Not fear of *him*. No matter what had passed between them, no matter how angry they had been with each other, she had never *feared* him.

But he was pushing them. Though, she had—she admitted to herself—started it by coming here. Perhaps she'd known that all along. Perhaps, in fact, that was what had brought her here. The truth of what had brought her here. Maybe all along she'd hoped that he would push her, that she would rile him enough to finally call her on it, in a way he'd never have dared to do while her grandfather was alive.

'Do you?' he asked her in return.

She nodded.

'I need to hear it, *mi amor*.'

The affectionate endearment made her want to growl, anger heating her cheeks with a flush, her antagonistic response enflaming his own.

'Yes,' she bit out from between clenched teeth.

'Undo your shirt,' he commanded, his voice guttural, the jump from hypothetical to real, to *happening*, lightning fast, dumping adrenaline and dopamine into her system, landing in the pulse points across her body.

He stepped back from her as if giving her space to do his bidding, his eyes heated and heavy on her body, waiting, impatient for her to reveal herself to him. His voyeurism spiked her pulse as she fought the natural inclination to refuse, to deny him. But to deny him would be to deny herself, and to deny the truth of what they had just agreed on. Because he was right. She did want this. She wanted this more than anything else in the world right now.

With one hand, she undid the button of the oyster silk shirt between her breasts. Micha's eyes were glued to every single move she made, making her feel the lie. Making her feel like she was precious to him, wanted beyond reason. The latter, she could just about believe.

She thought she might have rebelled under his scrutiny, but instead, she *delighted* in it. One by one, she freed the buttons, the heavy silk material slipping open, revealing skin barely covered only by the thin lace of the ivory basque she'd worn.

Her breasts felt heavy, aching from where his gaze

lingered, desperate for his touch, but he didn't move an inch. Was he holding himself back or was he that impervious to her?

No. He couldn't be. Everything in her roared in denial and the sudden need for proof that he wasn't.

She rolled her shoulders back, the loose silk that had been barely hanging on top of her body finally falling down her arms, pooling at her wrists. Not satisfied by the flush on the cut of his cheekbones, her fingers went to release the button of her trousers, before stepping out of them and shaking the shirt free.

Her pulse raced, her heart thudding in her chest as she stood there in her Louboutins and basque, needing him to react, needing to push him, just so that she could feel him push back. In the reflection of the glass behind Micha, she caught a glimpse of herself, standing there—proud, powerful and determined.

And more aroused than she had ever been in her *life*.

Oh god, she needed him to ease this want in her. She couldn't bear it any more. But if this was his plan…to get her to undress, and to not follow through, she might never recover. The thought needled into her brain, getting stuck, but just when she might have buckled under the fear of it, he moved.

He closed the distance between them in a blink of an eye. His lips took hers—there was no other way to describe it—took them, possessed them. His tongue plunged deep, filling her mouth, tangling with her own, and it was *magnificent*.

He swallowed her pleasure-drenched gasp, as his hands grasped her shoulders and drew her powerfully against him. With just the basque and his shirt, there was nothing to stop her from feeling the contours of his chest, of the muscles he hid beneath well-cut suits and layers of false sophistication.

Moans turned into whimpers and she was all but begging by the time he had finished the kiss.

'What is it you want, Maria? Tell me.'

'You,' she confessed.

And his hands roamed from her shoulders. One to her breast and one shockingly, over her backside, his palm caressing the curve of one cheek, fingers grabbing at her flesh. Damp wet heat pooled between her thighs and she bit her lip to stop the pleading, begging words that would have fallen if they'd been allowed.

She looked to him and saw one brow raised in knowing, knowing what she wanted and what she wouldn't admit to.

He shaped her thigh with the palm of his hand and hooked her leg over his hip, pressing her back against the wall and inserting himself between her legs in a way that left no further room for doubt. She bit her lip and moaned when she felt the ridge of his arousal at the juncture of her thighs, unable to regret the slip when he pushed against her, rubbing the aching bundle of nerves until she was shivering with want.

Maria's gasp was the most erotic thing Micha Rufina had ever heard and he couldn't hold himself back any more. He slipped a hand between them, his hand covering her core, the heel of his palm pressing against her clitoris in slow lazy circles that were the direct opposite of the way his pulse was raging beyond his control.

She shifted under her pleasure as if torn between wanting it and wanting to escape it, unaware that the tease was as much for himself as it was for her. Unable to resist any longer, he slipped a finger beneath the clasp of her basque, beneath the line of the dampened silk panties into hot slick flesh.

This time it was he who groaned out loud.

A shudder rolled between them and he was uncaring where it started from, who it started from.

Cazzo.

He shook his head, giving up the internal argument he'd been having with himself, and dropped to his knees. His hands swept around her trembling thighs, and he could hardly believe that was where he found himself. After so many years, so much denial…

But just the scent of her need for him drove all thought from his head.

'Micha.' His name on her tongue was a plea, a prayer.

He tore apart the clasps of the basque and inch by inch revealed the perfection of her as he pulled her panties down her legs. His heart thundered, punching at his ribcage. He was a ravaging beast hell-bent only on her pleasure. He parted her with one hand and reached to palm her breast with the other, as he took her core in an open-mouthed kiss, sinking into heaven.

He growled into her hot wet heat and she bucked against his mouth, as his tongue probed, plunged, filled and teased. Maria panted for air, as his palms claimed her backside, holding her to him as he devoured her with licks and sucks and nips and…

'Micha.' This time his name was a warning that he didn't need. He knew how close to orgasm she was. In part, because *he* was shockingly close to orgasm, and she hadn't even touched him. Her body, shaking and restless, her breath harsh and short, her hands clutching and grasping at his shoulders and his hair.

She was on the edge and he damn near loved it. *Loved* that she was as driven to the brink by him as she was. That she too was drowning under whatever this was.

'Micha, please,' she begged.

'No,' he said, against her clitoris, refusing to give her a quick release from this no matter how she whimpered, caught on the edge of an orgasm as sharp as it was sublime. He punished them by drawing out the painful pleasure that was killing them both.

'*Micha*,' she pleaded.

'No,' he said again, pressing his tongue against the small bundle of nerves and shaking his head as she shivered almost frantically now.

'Oh god,' she whispered, 'oh god.'

He lost count of her prayers, and instead indulged in the way her body readied itself for pleasure, the increase in heat, the dampness welling beneath his tongue, the way her legs tightened around him, the way that her cries became screams, and her breath got faster and faster, as he licked and nipped, and pressed and sucked, harder and harder, until everything stopped in a moment of shocked, tension-locked stillness… And then she collapsed against him in the ultimate surrender.

CHAPTER THREE

MARIA CAME BACK to herself, slowly. Breath by breath, her pulse thundering. Her body, almost painfully sensitive to everything around her, the light, the feel of the wall against her back, the neckline of her basque digging into the soft slopes of her breasts, and Micha. Between her legs, still, taking little sips from her that sent shock waves through her body again and again. Her hands were still fisted in his hair, her traitorous body doing its own thing, holding him to her.

She tried to think about what she'd done, but she couldn't because pleasure was still coursing through her body, carried thick and heavy in her bloodstream. She wasn't done, and she knew that Micha most definitely wasn't done. She'd felt the ridge of his arousal, through the superfine wool of his trousers. The powerful, steely length of him. And now she wanted *that*.

Micha Rufina had turned her into a sensual voracious monster and it didn't matter. Because after today, she would never see him again.

And rather than focusing on how that made her feel, she chose to focus on what that meant for her. On the fact that maybe, finally, she could take whatever she wanted from him. One final and only chance, to know what it was like, to explore everything she possibly could before never having to see him again.

It was liberating. It was freeing. She could do anything. She could *ask* for anything. Demand it. All the fantasies that he'd taunted her about. She could have them. This night. Oh, she knew he wouldn't deny her a single thing. Because he'd had fantasies too. She'd seen them in his eyes when he'd looked at her.

Her fingers flexed in his hair, before tugging him back. She looked down at him, at his mouth, glistening with her own desire. He licked his lower lip without taking his eyes from her and her heart pounded painfully in her chest.

He ran a thumb over the curve of his bottom lip, and drew himself from his knees to stand before her, forcing her to crane her head back to keep the eye contact that was driving her near wild with want.

'What?' she asked, trying to unearth the indefinable look in his gaze that was something like surprise. 'Did you think I'd leave now?'

'Yes,' he replied with the brutal honesty that had dominated their entire exchange that evening.

'I'm not leaving until this is well and truly done,' she said, the words landing like unexploded bombs between them.

'Are you sure, *cara*?' he asked, loosening the tie at his neck with two vicious yanks, her eyes hungering for the sight of a chest that had been impressive eleven years before but now would be incredible.

'Absolutely.'

'*Va bene*,' he replied, pulling his tie completely free with a snap.

Her fingers dug for purchase into the wall behind her

as he freed his shirt buttons, reversing the way that she had stripped for him earlier. He tugged the shirt free of his belted waist, as his eyes roamed downward from her face to her chest, her legs, her feet. She was achingly conscious she was still wearing her Louboutins, and in her undone basque she felt carnal. Erotic. The way his skin flushed as his gaze devoured her, made her feel dizzyingly high.

He shucked the shirt from his shoulders, and kicked off his shoes, toeing off his socks, and stood before her, his hands tackling the black leather belt with a ruthless efficiency that cracked the air as he removed it from his trousers.

The ridge of his arousal proud and powerful against the fine wool material, nothing self-conscious about him, he eased the taut material apart by flicking the button and releasing the zip just a touch. He stood bearing her scrutiny as she had borne his, presumably understanding her fascination, her desire. Not only to take in the changes of eleven years, but to relish the impact, the power it had on her. The dips and curves of his body, ones that she wanted to mould with her hands and her mouth, the way she imagined wrapping herself around him. *Wanting* to.

She left the security of the wall and stalked towards him, his gaze on her hers, his hands fisting at his sides, the only sign he was as affected by her as she was him. Instead of coming face to face with him, she circled around behind him. And finally she let herself *indulge*—perhaps unaware that it was easier for her to do so when he couldn't see the sheer enjoyment she took from his body.

Her fingers moulded and pressed into his shoulders, her lips tracing the trap muscles down from his neck, and towards the juncture of his waist. Her hands explored the sides of his chest and around the front, feeling their way across his abdomen and the hollow lines between his hips and the lower abdominals. She encased him perfectly to feel how he responded to her and she felt the breath lock in his chest, despite his taunting arrogant confidence.

His shoulders tensed against her breasts and, as her hands dipped lower, as she palmed him boldly over his trousers, the rumble of the growl in his throat sent shivers down her spine, the way he fought with himself not to push back against her hand and the fact that he had even done so. But she wanted him to lose that fight. Like she had. She wanted him desperate and begging. Pleading for release.

So, she came around to face him and just like he had, she dropped to her knees.

A string of curses turned the air a shocking vivid blue as he tried to stop her. But it was too late. This was what she wanted. What she'd always wanted.

She flicked his hands away and instead, slowly pulled the zipper down, parting the sides of his trousers and guiding them from his hips. The black briefs, close to his skin, cupped every single part of him lovingly, leaving absolutely nothing to the imagination. She bit her lip, a last moment of hesitation—not doubt, never doubt—before she swept those from around his waist, down over the musculature of his backside, and letting the hard, throbbing steel of him free. She took him in her hand first, the soft velvet of his skin so deceptive of the restrained power she knew, she *knew*, was there.

She gripped him gently, but firmly, as she lowered her fist to the base of him, the guttural exhale teasing her own arousal back to life. His hand fell to her shoulder, anchoring him, when she felt the tiny tremors across his body begin, and so it was with a smile that she took him into her mouth, closing around the blunt tip of his penis, and humming her pleasure around the thick, heavy, hot feel of him.

'Madonna mia.'

And honestly, Maria couldn't tell whether she'd thought it or he'd said it. He felt incredible in her mouth as she sucked and drew down on him. The power of what it did to him.

A hand fisted her hair, and she loved it—flexing and tightening, urging her on, or holding her back, it was a hardline into the wants and needs she'd never allow herself to voice.

His hips bucked, slowly at first, tentatively until she drove him ragged with teeth that gently and carefully scraped across the corona of his penis, her tongue testing the little nerve beneath it. The sound he made was unholy, sending fireworks across her skin and to her overly sensitised core.

More curses filled the air. *'Basta!'* he demanded, pulling away from her. It was small, but it was enough. But they both knew that he'd broken first. But she'd needed that, because he'd made her beg.

Oh, he was going to make her pay for that. It had taken absolutely everything in Micha to pull back from the brink of an orgasm that would have come far too hard and far too soon, and the sight of her still on her knees looking up at him, wide knowing eyes, was too damn much.

'Get up,' he ordered, turning his back, unable to keep looking at her like that and retain his control.

'Please,' she taunted from behind him and he cursed again, knowing that she'd stay right there until he said it.

On his lips, the word sounded feral, closer to a growl, but it was enough. He saw her rise to her feet in the reflection of the window. The low lighting of the penthouse office would have displayed them for all of Paris to see, if they hadn't been so far out of reach from any prying eyes.

But when he turned to find her standing in the middle of his office, barely covered by what remained of her basque, he thought for the first time that entire exchange that he'd seen a moment of vulnerability.

He nearly let loose the bitter laugh that filled his throat. She had no idea what she did to him. What he would do for her. What he had *done* for her. And before he could stop himself, he'd closed the distance between them and taken her in his arms and with his mouth. He'd swept her up against him, her thighs coming around his waist, ankles locking together, her hair tumbling around them in a cocoon.

'You don't want this, at any point,' he said between kisses that bruised and punished them equally, 'you stop. You say it. You tell me to stop,' he commanded.

'Like I'd have a problem with that,' she dismissed.

'This isn't a contest *cara*, I'm serious,' he said, flexing the grip on her thigh in warning.

He glared up at her, their dark gazes clashing and sparking, but she saw the moment the bravado fell away, and the tumble of tendrils shivered as she shook her head.

And that was all he needed before he walked them back towards the desk, placing her on the edge, and pushing everything from it onto the floor with a single sweep of his arm. She squeaked, starting in surprise, but he didn't care. He hungered for her. He always had. It had been too long and he knew that for as long as he lived, there would never be anyone like her for him. Never. She was it. She always had been. No matter how impossible it was and would always be. And if he was going to drown, then he would make sure that it would—for both of them—be *spectacular*.

Her hands reached for him before he could even take a breath, and he plucked his wallet from his pocket, retrieving the condom before tossing the wallet over his shoulder. He tore the foil packet open, her gaze hot and heavy on his every move, Maria biting her lip as he removed the condom and rolled the latex over his hardened length.

Her fingers shooed his hands away and she drew him to the cross-hatch of curls at the juncture of her legs, slowly guiding him between her folds, moaning in delight as she teased her clitoris with the head of his cock.

His fists flexed on the toned muscles of her thighs, spreading them wider, making more space for him. Her eyes opened straight onto his as she held him at her entrance. This was it. It was the furthest they had ever gone, back when they'd fooled around as teenagers barely understanding themselves, let alone another's body.

But things were different now. So very different, and without another thought, he slowly pushed into the hot wet welcoming heat of her, and *dio mio*, there were not enough words in the dictionary to describe this moment.

His head fell back, utterly surrendering to all that was sensation, that was Maria, that was what they could do together. Her shocked gasp expressed perfectly how stunned he was by this shared moment.

Micha swallowed. 'Should I—' He tried to engage his

brain to offer to stop when Maria told him absolutely not to stop if he wanted to survive the night.

Micha wasn't sure he would survive either way at this point. Her heels pressed him deeper into her from where they were braced against the backs of his thighs. Her internal muscles seized his erection and if he wasn't careful, he'd start shaking very soon. Slowly, inch by glorious inch, he pushed deeper and deeper, her breathy little moans all the encouragement he needed, until she had taken him to the hilt.

And he had to move, or she'd know. She'd know how at her mercy he truly was, and he couldn't have that. So, he pulled back halfway before thrusting powerfully back into her, her nails gouging his back, and the cry of pleasure in his ear all that he needed to do it again and again.

'Oh god,' she whimpered as she spread her legs wider to accommodate him and he couldn't not look, his heart thumping powerfully when he saw how they were joined, how she took him, how much she wanted him. Sweat beaded his brow and tension coiled in his balls and in the base of his spine.

Madonna mia, she drove him insane with want.

With what felt like one fist squeezing his erection and another a vice around his heart, all he could do was make it so that she'd never forget him, make it so incredible that she'd never think of another man again without comparing them to him. If she was going to be written on his heart for the rest of his life, then she deserved the same.

Maria had never, *could* never, have imagined it would be like this. And while he drowned her in a pleasure so sensual, so *generous*, he could never know that it was her first time. That he was her one and only and always had been. She couldn't ever let him know that. Because if he did, he'd know the power he had over her. The lengths that she'd gone to, to preserve whatever dignity and power she had, would be all but destroyed. And she couldn't have that. But also, she couldn't *not* have this. Because this was...

He moved again, slowly pushing deeper into her, and the moan that fell from her lips was nothing short of erotic. Her head fell back and one hand palmed her breast as the other was around her backside, pulling her to the edge of the table, pulling her onto him.

On to him. *Oh god.* Her internal muscles flexed around the hardened length of his arousal.

There had been a moment at the very beginning where it had hurt, the sting of his intrusion, the unfamiliarity of it, that had locked her breath in her lungs and silenced her words. But so quickly it had transformed into something else, something softer, hotter, building into pleasure, to passion, building to a craving that she couldn't imagine, yet instinctively knew.

Her body reacted purely on instinct, her nails digging and grasping for him, for more, with him so deep within her, she wasn't sure where she ended and he began. And while a part of her thought that it shouldn't be like this with him, it shouldn't be this magical with a man who had all but broken her heart so long ago, a silent, more primal, more intuitive part of her had always known it would be like this.

He reached between them, his thumb pressing against her clitoris, pushed into applying pressure by the thrusts of his hips, the tilt of her pelvis, her body greedy for all that she could take from this one and only time she'd ever have with him. If she had to fit a lifetime of pleasure into this one moment, then damn it, she would.

'Lie back for me,' he ordered and, cheeks flushing at the command in his voice, the only one she'd allow him to give, she did. Her body shifted into the new position as he hooked one of her legs over his shoulder, the way that her heart pounded in time with each thrust of his hips as he slid even deeper into her reaching a part of her that simply imploded.

Out of nowhere, she was hit by an avalanche of pleasure. It slid over her, burying her, muting the world in a thick, hot blanket in the single space between heartbeats. Her body bucked and twisted as Micha found his release at the same time, the pulsing and clenching of their joined bodies prolonging a pleasure so intense it was near torturous.

She wanted to laugh, to cry, as if the pleasure had burst through all the barriers that had been holding back her emotions for months, for *years*. But she didn't want any of that. She didn't want to feel those things. She just wanted... Oh, she didn't know any more. She bit her lip, trying to pull everything back before Micha could see.

He was braced over her, his head bent over her heaving chest, his own breaths powerful punches that she felt all over her body. The only thing that made this, any of this, okay was that he seemed as affected as her. That they had at least, finally, been equals, brought low by themselves, rather than each other.

His body heated hers as her skin began to cool, as realisation began to dawn and as doubts crept in. She needed to get away. She needed to regroup. She needed to get dressed, deeply discomforted by her vulnerability in her present state.

Micha leaned back up, away from her, his dark gaze searching hers, his eyes containing as many questions and as much confusion as she felt in that moment.

She opened her mouth to speak, but he took one final advantage of her and claimed her mouth with his. He didn't need to. They'd already shared what they were going to. But for some reason the kiss soothed just a little of the ragged hurt beginning to build. That he still wanted her, after everything. That he needed what she needed.

The kiss was raw, guttural, a tangle of teeth and tongue, of fisted hands and grasping fingers, and over far, far too soon.

'Stay there,' he said, as he gently left her body, pulling his trousers up over his hips and stalking over to a door at the back of the room.

Maria waited until he was gone, before lurching up off the table, and searching for her clothes. No way would she stay there waiting for him like one of his Parisian girls. She grasped her shirt from where she'd thrown it over a chair, found her trousers on the opposite side of the room. She was just about to put them on when Micha re-emerged into the room holding a small cloth in his hands.

'I should have known you wouldn't listen.'

Maria clenched her jaw, her gaze flicking to the cloth he'd brought for her. The touch, the care, the thought all more than she wanted to consider right now.

'Why would I start now?' she bit back, realising that the small room he'd been in must have been a bathroom. She clutched her clothes to her chest and passing him, she plucked the cloth from his hands, taking herself into the small en suite, ignoring what she thought might have been a growl.

Micha flexed and released his fists, frustrated that she wouldn't even let him care for her after what they'd shared. They didn't have to like each other for that, but she wouldn't even let him do that. Cristo, he'd taken her like an animal. He'd been as lost to Maria as his mother had been to the addiction that she'd spent her entire life fighting.

That's what made Maria such a risk. That she had, and always would, be the one thing that he could lose himself to. But Gio had been right. She wasn't meant for him. Not then. And certainly not now.

He stalked over to where his shirt had lain beneath hers and shrugged into it, doing up the buttons, one by one, reclaiming the cool, near icy-cold detachment he was known for. No one would have believed him capable of the kind of loss of control he'd just experienced with the granddaughter of his mentor and guide. But he'd always known, hadn't he?

He just wished to god he hadn't been so right.

Maria emerged from the bathroom behind him, not even a hair out of place. She looked as if she'd just conducted the most boring audit in the world, and he felt...

Wrecked.

'Maria—'

'This changes nothing. I still expect you to be out of here by the time the ink dries on my marriage certificate.'

Micha bit back a string of invectives that would have

burned the entire building down, instead simply saying, 'Of course.'

There was so much he wanted to say, but nothing emerged from the steel band clamped around his heart. She didn't want to hear it and he didn't have the ability to say it.

She nodded once, more to herself, and brushed past him with barely a second glance, the ice-cold breeze rolling off her making him shiver. He tucked his shirt in to the waist of his trousers and pulled up the zip, turning to her, half outraged, half furious and beyond unimpressed.

'You're going to leave? Just like that?' he said, shocked enough to finally speak.

'Why not? You did,' she accused, and for the barest of moments, he thought he saw it. The sheer incandescent hurt that he sometimes thought she might be hiding. But then she blinked and it was gone, part of his imagination, a hangover from the young girl he'd once known.

'You know it wasn't that simple,' he replied.

'Seemed pretty cut and dry to me,' she said, reaching for the purse that had ended up by the door to the office. 'Which suited me just fine,' she said, adjusting the strap of her purse over her shoulder, near eviscerating him with her carelessness.

'What was this?' he asked. 'Really? Was it you just getting what you wanted?' he forced himself to ask, hating that weakness in him that needed to know.

'I got the only thing you were ever good for, Micha,' she bit out and stalked from his life leaving burn marks across his skin and soul.

Maria held it together, all the way down the corridor, in the lift she knew was covered by CCTV, and out onto the streets of Paris. She held it together while the chauffeur-driven car took her back to the private airfield where the Gallo Group's jet was ready for take-off. She waited until they were forty-one thousand feet in the air before going to the bathroom where no one could see or hear her, and shattering into a million pieces, knowing that she would never, not ever, be the same again.

CHAPTER FOUR

Three months later...

TO SAY THAT Micha Rufina was pissed off was an understatement of near epic proportions. The last place and person he ever thought he'd be, or *wanted* to be, on his way to see was Maria Gallo. And if he'd had a say in the matter, he'd have never laid eyes on her again as long as he lived. But no one could have predicted what had happened after Maria had left Paris that last, fateful night.

Not even Gio Gallo.

Antonio Gallo, despite his promise to his cousin Maria, had *not* divorced the wife he'd married six years ago for convenience and instead chosen to remain with Ivy for love. Meaning that he and Maria failed to meet the terms of Gio Gallo's will and less than two weeks after she had left Paris, the entirety of Gallo Group had passed into Micha's hands, setting off what the world's press had termed the biggest Italian bloodbath since the second Mafia wars of the 1980s.

Family had turned on family, threats both physical and legal had been made, retracted and made again. Stocks had plummeted and recovered, risen and tumbled in various different ways until everyone realised that the world *hadn't* in fact collapsed under Micha's ruthless and—surprising to some—*expert* control.

Which was why Micha was absolutely furious that he was now on his way to see Maria because one single client, one out of thousands spread out across the world, refused to continue to do business with Gallo Group unless *she* handled the renewed contract negotiations.

It had been on the tip of his tongue to tell the client that he could go and get incredibly creative with notions of self-pleasure, were it not for the fact that they were GG's biggest international client and if they lost that client, it could very well start a mass exodus that Gallo Group literally *wouldn't* survive. This one client would be the proverbial straw.

He checked his watch as his driver took the turn towards Sant'Arcangelo, and frowned. He lowered the screen between them and said, 'Why are we heading south?'

'We are going to Signora Gallo, *si*?'

'*Si*. Is she no longer in Arezzo with her mother?'

'Signora Gallo moved recently. It is the same distance timewise,' the driver said, misunderstanding the motivation behind his query.

'*Va bene*,' Micha replied, raising the screen again.

Why had she moved? And when?

Things had been so crazy in the last four months, but this was an alarming reminder that he could not afford to let things slip through his fingers. Like Maria, moving out of her parents' estate and to the middle of nowhere. He had known that she'd have been furious at losing the company, but he hadn't expected her to quit.

Even before the announcement that Micha would be

returning to Rome headquarters to assume the position of company president and CEO, Maria had submitted her resignation.

And now this hermit-like move? It was the exact opposite of the fight he'd expected to have with her and he'd been left strangely bereft by it. There must be something else going on. He had approximately forty-five minutes left to arm himself with as much information as he could. But when he checked Maria's socials, there was resounding silence. No posts, no updates, nothing about her house move. Nothing since the day before Antonio informed her and the family of his decision to remain married to Ivy. Micha had checked Antonio's pages too, in case there was a reference to Maria by proxy, but nothing.

Which was why by the time he arrived at the small villa hugging the shoreline of Lake Trasimeno, he was as curious as he was frustrated, and in an even worse mood than he'd been when he disembarked Gallo Group's private jet.

Micha stepped out of the tinted-windowed car, slipping on his sunglasses and looking around at Maria Gallo's new abode. He surveyed the old farm-style villa, narrow and, unusually, all one storey. The stone walls were rough, but familiar, the light mortar making the terracotta and grey stones appear bright in the morning sunlight. But despite the evident age of the building, the roof was new, tiles gleaming, and the hints of modernisation were subtle but expensive. He could just about see the corner of a small green garden from where he stood, brushing up against the side of Lake Trasimeno.

What on earth was she doing out here? It wasn't exactly nowhere, but it wasn't the bustling, busy, swanky city address that he knew she'd loved so much. Because Maria thrived on busy, on the frenetic energy that surrounded her. It fed her and made her happy. This?

This looked a hell of a lot like exile and he didn't like it one bit.

But he didn't have to like it, he reminded himself. This was hers and it had nothing to do with him. All he was here for was to convince her to sweet-talk a client back into the fold and then she could leave. Oh, he wasn't an imbecile—he knew she'd make him work for it. Nor was he a complete bastard. He'd give her a nice hefty commission for doing it. But once that was done, they could go back to their respective corners of Italy and never cross paths again as far as he was concerned.

Liar, his inner voice taunted, reminding him of the sensual turmoil he'd been in ever since she'd left his office in Paris three months previous.

Shifting his sunglasses on to his head only for the brief moment he took to pinch the bridge of his nose, he attempted to wrestle his wayward body back under his control.

It was no use denying it. He'd been tormented every single night with fantasies that had built on what they'd shared that stolen night and spun them wildly into erotic fever dreams. Each night he woke, bed sheets sweat soaked, heart pounding, head aching and fiercely unsatisfied.

Maybe seeing her would purge her from his memory. Show him that he had blown that moment far out of proportion because of their history. That there was no reason for him to still be lusting after a woman who thought him little better than dirt beneath her high-heeled shoe.

And with that thought, determination imprinted on his mind, he lowered his sunglasses to his eyes, turned and went to knock on the door of Maria Gallo.

Maria eyed the red-soled heels and sighed before reluctantly putting them away. She wouldn't be needing those now, or any time soon for that matter. And she knew it was silly to get so emotional about a shoe, but it wasn't really about the shoe, was it?

She'd been unpacking box by box, day by day following Ivy's suggestion when Maria told her about the move. She knew that Ivy and Antonio felt truly awful about what happened. And Maria *loved* that Antonio had found true happiness with his wife. And having met Ivy, Maria couldn't blame him. The English woman was exactly the kind of person Maria would have picked for him. She was beautiful and smart and funny, and she made her cousin laugh. And Ivy had been utterly devastated that their happiness had cost Maria Gallo Group.

She *knew* that Antonio deserved that happiness. It was just that she hated that it had come at the cost of what *she* deserved but had never been deemed worthy of.

Gallo Group.

Her heart twisted and something that felt a lot like grief welled within her.

Maria's resignation hadn't been knee-jerk. It had been her only option. There was absolutely no way that she could have stayed at GG once it went to Micha. Not after what happened in Paris. And certainly not after the consequences of that night either.

Shaking off the thoughts that threatened to pull her in a thousand different directions, she pushed the storage box into the large cupboard containing the other clothes she'd not been able to part with. Clothes had meant so much to her over the years. They'd been her armour, her protectors while she'd worked at Gallo Group. They'd helped her to feel the confidence she'd faked until it felt a little less…fake.

But that part of her life was over now. She had lost Gallo Group. And the family that had never thought she was good enough for it in the first place, now held her solely responsible for the fact that it had slipped into the hands of…of…

Maria swallowed whatever feeling it was that thickened her throat. That was another unpacked box she'd brought with her from the move to this beautiful farm house on Lake Trasimeno, albeit an emotional one.

She looked out of the wall of glass that had been the true selling point of the recently renovated one-storey villa; the slash of placid blue reminding her of the calm that she was going to need. Especially now.

Micha. She should never have gone to see him. She should never have thought herself immune to him. But she had so desperately wanted him to see what he had abandoned all those years ago. She had so desperately wanted to see regret in his eyes. But all she'd seen was the ferocity of his want.

Her phone flashed with a message.

I'll be done in about ten mins and call you then? Ivy xx

Ivy had been a lifesaver. As unlikely as it seemed, Maria and Antonio's wife had formed a fast and firm friendship. And since Ivy and Antonio had returned from

London and had spent the past few months in Antonio's Tuscan villa, Maria had seen more of them than anyone else.

And, if Maria was honest, she would need that friendship more than ever, because in six months' time it wouldn't just be her, she thought, sweeping a hand over her stomach. Especially since her father's reaction was less than understanding.

How could you be so stupid?
Who was it? Who did this to you.
And when she'd refused to tell him?
You're no better than a whore.

Maria swallowed, forcing herself to remember her father's last words. Because as much as they hurt, they also steeled her backbone. Made her determined. Determined never to be beholden to a man ever again.

Because for all her apparent independence, her managerial position at GG, her eye-watering—and wholly justifiable—salary and for all the power she'd *thought* she'd had, her father had still turned up at her mother's house and kicked her out of a home he hadn't lived in for over fifteen years.

And he could. Because, as he pointed out, *he* owned it.

She'd looked at the mother who had betrayed her secret and saw the guilt in her eyes, but the fear in them too when she glanced at the husband who hadn't been a husband for that same number of years. In that moment, Maria had realised that although they had lived in separate houses since Maria was eight years old, they only really saw each other at family events, where they played the image of a happy family, despite the fact that *the entire family* knew they were anything but, her mother had never really escaped her husband's rule or wallet. Her mother would *always* defer to her husband, even at the cost to her daughter.

So, in the space of six weeks, Maria lost her job, her family and her home. And no one had said a single thing.

The only thing that had kept her father quiet about her pregnancy was shame.

And what had kept *her* quiet? Fear. Maybe she was more like her mother than she cared to be. But could she really afford to be that way? Especially now?

Maria thought back to that day when Ivy found her red eyed and shocked and forced her to tell her what was going on. At first, Maria had thought the reason her period was two months late was down to stress. But one pregnancy test after another had told her differently.

She was going to be a mother. The realisation had filled Maria with so much emotion, and so many thoughts, she hadn't known where or how to begin sorting through them all.

In the meantime, she had sworn Ivy to secrecy, and she had only agreed because she—like Maria—knew that the first thing Antonio would do was to track Micha down and beat the living daylights out of him. But Ivy's agreement had come with a two-month time limit and that time was running out.

Butterflies fluttered in Maria's stomach and she once again soothed the slight swell of her abdomen.

At twelve weeks, she'd been told, the baby was now fully formed, and about the size of a lime. Her baby. Her and Micha's baby. And although it was probably hyperbole, she was convinced that they could feel everything, experience everything, vicariously. And *oh god*, she didn't want her child to grow up like she had, with a father who was mean and a mother who was a mouse. She wanted… more. She wanted love, security, confidence. She didn't want them to grow up fighting for their place in the world, but sure of it. She wanted…

She felt the tear roll down her cheek and swept it away. It didn't matter what she wanted, Maria thought determinedly, sweeping aside foolish hopes and dreams just as easily as her tears. She might have left Rome, she might have left Gallo Group, but she was still the practical, focused woman she had become. That didn't change just because she was going to be a mother. A single, unwed mother.

Zia Alessina had done it, after divorcing her husband to bring up Antonio on her own. And this was decades later. It was the twenty-first century. And although she firmly believed that she didn't need a piece of paper to make herself socially acceptable, she was devastated that her child might bear the burden of that decision.

This was the problem with her thoughts. Back and forth they swung, like a pendulum, hovering a bare millimetre over the biggest emotional box there was; the one with Micha Rufina's name scrawled on the side.

Oh, she *would* tell him—she'd never keep that secret either from her child or him. But she needed to make a plan first. She needed to make sure that she had security and her independence. Because if he found out that she was pregnant with his child… If he had even the slightest inkling… He'd come in and take over. Force them to do something inconceivably foolish like get married.

And then she'd *never* be free. And she just wanted so much to be free.

The thought rushed out of her on a sigh as she looked down at the large black bag of things she'd decided not to take with her into her future. Wasn't this part of her freedom? Not being weighed down with things that no longer served her? She probably should have done it before she moved, but there hadn't been time. She'd thrown everything she had into the back of cars as her father hurled abuse at her for bringing shame on the family.

She dragged the bag out of the spare room, down the corridor that opened into the large open-plan living, dining and kitchen area, and up to the front door. She'd throw this out and get rid of the bad energy of her thoughts at the same time. No more business suits that she didn't need, she decided as she put the bag down to open the door, no more thoughts of her father, she told herself as she unlocked the bolt at the top, pulling open the door, and no more...

Micha Rufina.

His hand raised to knock on the door, he was as surprised as Maria looked when she opened the door to find him standing there. But the last thing he expected was for her to slam it shut again.

He blinked.

Really? She was *that* childish.

He waited. And then waited some more, getting even more annoyed. And if things continued like this, he'd have a heart attack from sheer irritation.

'Maria, *per favore*, open the door,' he called. 'It's not like you can ignore me.'

Her silence objected to his statement.

'Maria?' He blew out a breath, ignoring the weight of

the driver's gaze from within the air-conditioned blacked-out-windowed town car.

'Maria Aurora Guilia Gallo, open this door!' he yelled.

'I am not a child and you don't get to talk to me like I am one, just because you are now officially the boss of everything,' she fired back angrily through the door, in a—to his mind—very childish way.

'*Madonna mia*, Maria, open the damn door,' he said. The way the alliteration rolled around his mouth was familiar; tasting like affection, frustration and grief all at the same time. He was trying to parse his way through those feelings when she opened the door looking mutinous and absolutely glorious.

Dio, it was a punch to his chest that knocked the air from his lungs and he was thankful that he was at least wearing his sunglasses to hide behind.

Thick dark curls tumbled around her face, her cheeks flush with indignation, her eyes sparkling with fury and all he could think of was how she looked when she orgasmed and he forced himself to look away before he made a fool of himself.

'Why are you here?' she demanded, a large bin bag placed on the ground between them.

'I'd rather not have this conversation on the doorstep.'

'I'd rather not be having this conversation at all, but here we are,' she shot back.

He slipped his thumb and forefinger beneath the frame of his glasses and pinched his nose again. The tension headache that bracketed his temples was just getting worse and worse. He really didn't need this. He had very little time, maybe less than twenty-four hours to save the contract, and then get back to the rest of Gallo Group.

'I need to speak to you about the Peterson account.'

'Peterson? You need to... You're here because...' Her tongue swept out across her bottom lip before she pulled it beneath her teeth.

'What did you think I'd be here for?' Micha demanded, confused.

Maria huffed out a bitter laugh and honestly? He didn't know what was going on. Because she was the one who had quit after all. He'd have willingly continued to work with her because she was excellent at her job. And there was a small petty part of him that felt that Gallo Group might *not* have been in such a precarious position if she hadn't quit.

'Nothing. Absolutely nothing,' she said, answering his question, turning her back on him and disappearing into the house, leaving Micha to move the bag blocking the doorway so that he could follow her.

He walked into a large open-plan space that somehow managed to be both open and full of light, and yet cosy and calm. It was significantly different to the property she and her mother had lived in before Maria had left Rome.

That had been dark, cluttered with books, paintings and expensive trinkets. Old money, with no taste was how he'd once thought of it, when he'd been there for one of the family gatherings. He'd never visited it when he and Maria had...

He shut that thought down and followed her towards the kitchen, letting her put the long marble-top island between them for distance and safety.

She avoided his gaze, fussing with coffee cups and the sleek machine that vibrated at an impossibly quiet hum. He watched her choose decaf and frowned. He was about to say something when she interrupted his train of thought.

'What did you do?' she said, her tone accusing but curious, as if in spite of herself.

'What do you mean?' he asked, confused.

'To Peterson. That account was safe, the client was happy. And you can't afford to lose Peterson right now.'

'Why do you think *I* did something?' he bit out, angry at the assumption that he had somehow messed up, and choosing to ignore the warning that he was already very much aware of.

'Because Peterson was happy. And now he's not.'

Micha rubbed his jaw. 'He wants you to handle the contract renewal.'

'I don't work there any more,' Maria said and he waved her statement aside with his hand.

She narrowed her gaze at him.

'What did you *do*?'

'It was an admin error,' he explained.

'What was?'

'Contracts used an outdated template, and Peterson thought I was trying to pull a fast one. He says the trust is broken and the only person he'll deal with is you.'

'An admin error? And management didn't think to check it?'

'In case you hadn't noticed, we've been a little busy in the last few months,' he bit out angrily.

'Poor you,' Maria bit back as she plonked his espresso before him, barely managing to keep the coffee in the cup.

As he took a sip, she shook her head.

'No.'

He had expected her to put up a fight. And he had come prepared. 'I—'

'No, Micha.'

'You haven't heard my offer yet.'

'It won't matter.'

'You'll be a consultant, and you'll get an on-signing bonus worth ten percent of the contract,' he explained.

'No,' she said again.

'Fine. I'll give you your job back with an increase in salary, and a promotion to senior vice-president.'

'No.'

'What?' he replied, genuinely shocked.

His offer was more than generous. It was so good it was almost bad business. And she would have known that. And she was still saying no? And even if it *wasn't* good enough, surely the risk to a company that was as good as her lifeblood would be enough to get her on board.

'There is literally nothing that you could offer me that would make me come back to Gallo Group and work under you. It's yours. You handle it. And if that's all?'

Micha frowned, bracing against the punch of her words. He thought that she'd play hardball. That she'd take some convincing, but this flat-out refusal, this wasn't stubbornness. Because he knew what stubbornness looked like on her. This didn't even have the heat of outrage or anger. This was cold. This was...*numb*.

'If you've finished your coffee, I'd like you to leave.'

He clenched his jaw, stifling all the arguments and objections, the questions that thickened his throat. There was something going on here. She was definitely trying to get rid of him. But why?

Her mobile rang just as he was going to press his point,

and she let it ring as she stared at him until he raised his hands in surrender.

'Va bene.'

She reached for her phone, and asked Antonio's wife to give her two minutes. He'd seen Ivy's name flash up on the screen.

Maria gestured for him to return to the door.

'You can see yourself out,' she said, turned her back on him and looked out through the large window that formed the back wall of the open-plan room.

He had been dismissed and he didn't like it one bit.

'Ivy... No, not at all. How are you doing?' he heard Maria ask in English.

Turning on his heel, he walked to the door. He wasn't going to beg her to come back. Yes, he needed her. But if Gallo Group had to continue without Peterson, he'd do that. But...it wasn't Peterson that had him curious now. It was Maria.

He closed the door behind him and stepped out into the sunshine.

Something wasn't right. He'd seen her furious, with him, he'd seen her grieving over Gio, he'd seen her pleasured and he'd seen her happy. He'd never seen her so... closed down. As if she was trying to hide something. But what?

Maria cast a look over her shoulder, her heart pounding in her chest and blood rushing in her ears.

'Are you okay?' Ivy asked, worried, after Maria had explained that Micha was there. 'How did he know where you are?'

'Someone must have told him,' Maria surmised.

'Maria, I'm not sure about this. I really think I need to tell Antonio,' Ivy wavered.

'Please don't,' Maria begged. 'Please. I just… I just need a little more time. And if Antonio found out, all hell would break loose.'

'Perhaps it *should* break loose.'

'Ivy!'

'Sorry. I just think that this is too much for you to be dealing with on your own.'

'It's a lot, I know, believe me. But I just need some time. I need a plan. I need…' Oh, she didn't really know what she needed.

Maria walked, unsettled, back through the house to the room where she'd been packing up her things. Her heart was still racing from having Micha here, in her home. He'd looked so…*good.* And so tired.

A part of her had felt victorious about the Peterson account. That Micha was struggling to hold Gallo Group together. And that was a mean part of her. But honestly, it had been a dream of hers for him to come begging at her door, to tell her that he needed her. To beg for her help. For weeks, months even, she'd fantasised about him doing just that.

So, how ironic was it that she'd had to say no? That she'd not even been able to take up his offer and prove just how vital she was to Gallo Group? Because she couldn't. Negotiations would take at least two months, and by then…by then she'd be showing. And she wasn't sure that even then she'd be ready…

She swept a protective hand over her abdomen. Very few people could have guessed that she was pregnant at this moment. Would the father of her child have been one of them?

'Ivy, if he finds out...' Maria shuddered at the thought, unable to even finish the sentence. 'I just need some time. And then, when I'm ready, I'll tell Micha.'

'Tell me what, *cara*?'

Maria spun round in shock, coming face to face with Micha.

'I saw you leave,' she whispered in horror.

'Well, I came back,' he said, grim faced and hard eyed. 'And now, I think it's time that you tell me exactly what's going on, whether you're ready or not.'

His gaze bored into hers, flicked down to where her hand was on her abdomen, and rose back up to hers, eyes widening, lips parting in shock.

'You're pregnant.'

CHAPTER FIVE

IT WAS THE nightmare that had haunted her for the last two months, come to life. Micha stood there, eyes wide, knowing, accusing, confusion, anger, and something she couldn't quite name, swirling in the rich gaze boring into her.

'Maria? Are you okay? Maria?'

Ivy's voice sounded so very distant.

'I have to go,' Maria whispered into the phone.

'If I don't hear from you in twenty minutes I'm telling Antonio,' Ivy warned.

Maria ended the call without taking her eyes off Micha.

'You're pregnant,' he said again. 'You're… We're…'

He looked as if he'd been sucker-punched.

'We used protection. We…' he trailed off again.

He looked, Maria thought, the way she probably had looked when she'd found out too. Shock, confusion, denial, *fear*. His eyes dropped again to her stomach and she wanted to put her hands there, to protect their child, not from *him*, but from what would now happen.

She braced herself for the question. For the hurt that would wash over her. For the accusations and denials. For the shouts and the recriminations. But instead, he turned on his heel and left.

What?

Her outraged gasp echoed in the empty room. He *left*?! How *dare* he leave her again?

Fury had her chasing him back down the corridor.

'Where are you going?' she demanded, a blinding anger pouring through her veins at the thought that he would leave her, leave *them*.

She came into the living area and saw him yanking his tie loose with three firm pulls. He shucked out of his suit jacket and rolled up his sleeves, as if he was just about to get started, rather than depart. He anchored one hand on his hip, as the other flew to fist his thick, dark hair, apparently utterly ignorant of how the sight of him like that melted both her insides and her brain at the same time.

Maybe it was the pregnancy she thought. Maybe—

'Have you had the tests and the scans?' he asked, his question pulling her thoughts back to the room but not in a direction she had expected.

She swallowed before answering. 'Yes.'

He closed his eyes for a beat. 'Is everything…?' She thought she almost heard his breath shudder in his lungs, and she realised that he was worried.

'Everything is fine,' she rushed to reassure him.

He nodded, only opening his eyes after. Something in his gaze turned then. She suppressed the urge to shiver. There was a coldness there that she'd never once seen in him all those years ago. Age and experience had put that there, and for just a moment, she regretted it.

'And you answered all their questions? About the medical history?' he asked, bringing her back to the present.

On the surface his tone was polite, but there was something cold about the question. She ignored the warning signs, irritated instead by the implication that she would have already messed something up. Just like everyone had always expected of her. Just like she had done with GG.

'Of course I did,' she replied.

'Family history?'

'Yes, Micha. I gave them my family history too.'

'And mine?' he asked. 'What information did you give them about *my* family history?' he demanded, his tone morphing from polite to pointed in the space of a heartbeat. 'Would you have told them about my mother's gestational diabetes?'

Her thoughts crashed to a halt.

'I don't think that has any—' Maria hesitated.

'You don't *think*? Well, that's medically accurate, Maria.'

'I didn't know,' she confessed, shamefaced.

'You didn't *know* because you didn't *ask*, because you didn't tell me!' he shouted.

'I didn't tell you because I thought you would force me to marry you,' she shouted back.

'Oh, we *will* be getting married, Maria,' Micha declared with such supreme confidence it was maddening.

'Why do you think it is yours?' she struck out.

'Are you going to lie to me and tell me it's not?' he retorted.

'No,' she admitted reluctantly. She ground her teeth together, hating that he knew her so well. Hating that he knew she wouldn't resort to lies.

'Then such dramatics are unnecessary,' he said with infuriating cold-hearted logic. 'We will marry.'

'No, we won't.'

'Yes, we will,' he insisted.

Maria threw her hands up in the air and turned her

back to him, just to get a moment's reprieve. He did this to her. Made her so feel so mad, so ungrounded…so *exposed*.

'How long have you known?' he asked from behind her.

And this time it was she who closed her eyes. He would never forgive her for keeping something like this from him. She'd known it from the moment she'd decided she needed to.

'I needed time, Micha,' she tried to explain.

'How long?'

'One month.'

His shock was a gasped exhale.

'Were you…?' He seemed to brace himself against the question on the tip of his tongue. 'Were you waiting until…because you thought I would…?'

Realisation cut through her like a knife and she spun around to face him. 'No, Micha. No,' she rushed to reassure him. Whatever she felt about what had passed between them, whatever she thought about what he had done to her, she'd never have thought that he would try to convince her to terminate the pregnancy. Because while she didn't know the man he had become, she knew the boy he had been.

He might have spent the last eleven years in Paris doing god knows what, but that didn't mean she didn't know him, hadn't grown up with him, hadn't seen the way he was with his mother, with the people he considered his, family, friends. The people that Micha considered his were protected in a way that went almost beyond necessary.

But how could she explain that it was that very thing

that she'd feared would stifle her? Would do more harm to her than anything else?

He looked deep into her eyes, searching for the truth in her words. His second shuddered exhale she felt down to her bones and that was when she felt truly sorry that she'd kept their pregnancy from him. Before it was so quickly masked, she saw the wound her secret had inflicted upon him. The doubts and insecurities she had forgotten in the years spent apart from him.

And for the first time a dust-covered memory floated free. Micha, aged sixteen, boyish and nervously charming, signs of the man he would become beneath his skin. Hints of the flirtation that would become something more in barely a few months' time, as they shared whispers of futures that they wanted. She'd told him about wanting to take over Gallo Group one day and he'd insisted she would. And when he'd haltingly confessed that he wanted a family, she'd told him she could see it, secretly hoping that perhaps it was something they could have together.

And here they were, nearly twelve years later and...

It was all so very wrong.

How had everything gone so wrong? Micha wondered, as he glared out the window at the placid lake, feeling anything but.

He was going to be a father.

Madonna mia.

He swept a hand through his hair in a way that he wanted to do with his life. He should have left, instead of coming into the living area and planting his feet. He needed time to marshal his thoughts. He felt it, the heady complex chaos of his thoughts filling his mind and stopping his tongue to a point of near silence.

There's no problem. It just takes Micha longer than most to connect his words to his thoughts, the doctor had said when Gio had dragged him there, wanting to make sure there was no 'problem' with the sixteen-year-old who would become his right-hand man. Most had thought that his monosyllabic tendencies were down to either limited intelligence or stubbornness, but Gio had known from the beginning that there was nothing unintelligent about him. He just needed a little time, and a little encouragement to separate out his thoughts from his feelings.

But he didn't have time. Not now, he thought, pushing aside the familiar nauseating panic that threatened to clog his throat. He needed to think. And quickly. Because if he didn't get this right, he knew, he *knew*, Maria would wriggle out of his clasp and disappear. And he couldn't let that happen.

He was going to be a father.

He, who had never known anything but violence, fear and abandonment from his own. It was true that once, so long ago now he could almost think it unreal, he'd wanted a family. But that was before. Before he had learned that such things were not meant for a man like him.

Because no matter how far he climbed out of the gutter, it was still there: the dirt on his hands that meant he'd never be good enough. Certainly not for Maria Gallo. Only now, there was no choice in the matter.

She had known for a month and she hadn't told him? The realisation hit him like a freight train, dredging up the question from the deepest part of his soul. The part that had clung fiercely to a relationship that was long since gone.

'Would you have told me?' he demanded.

Maria looked at the floor.

'Yes. Eventually,' she said in surrender. 'I just wanted… time. Everything changed, Micha. Everything I thought I knew, everything I thought would be, it's all gone and this,' she said, sweeping a hand over a bump that was barely there, 'this happened and I just… I wanted time.'

He, of all people, understood and knew that feeling. He could appreciate the quiet desperation in her words. He really could. But they didn't have the luxury of time. And he didn't have the luxury of being nice.

'Well, that time is up,' he said, pulling out his phone and firing off a message to his assistant cancelling all meetings.

'What are you doing?' she asked, hooking her foot behind the ankle of her standing leg. She'd used to do that when she was younger, he remembered. When she was nervous. He dismissed the sight of it and went back to his emails.

'I'm cancelling all my meetings.'

'What about Peterson?' she asked, causing his head to snap up.

He blinked. Once. Twice.

Then he huffed out a bitter laugh, his eyes roaming the room, before coming back to her, in disbelief.

'Really? That's what you're worried about right now?' he demanded. Of course she would care more about Gallo Group than, oh, just a little something like telling him he was the father of an unborn child.

'Well, that's what brought you here,' she pressed. 'You said you needed me to handle the contract renewal.'

'It doesn't matter. I'll deal with it later,' he dismissed.

'You can't. He's GG's biggest client. If he goes, then the whole company will fall apart!' she exclaimed.

And he knew he shouldn't be surprised. He knew he shouldn't be angry that at this very moment in time, just when he was struggling with the fact that he was going to be a father, *she* was worrying about her family's damn company.

'This is very true,' he agreed. 'It's also something you didn't care one single iota about less than twenty minutes ago. And as you so rightly pointed out, Gallo Group is mine and I'll handle it in the way I see fit.'

She let out a growl of frustration that matched precisely how he felt. He locked his phone screen, slipping it back into his pocket, and watched as Maria did a very good impression of someone about to throw a tantrum. He imagined there would be only three seconds before she started tapping her foot on the floor in annoyance. That she did it in four seconds showed a surprising amount of restraint on her behalf. She huffed a long wave of thick black curls over her shoulder and his hand fisted from the memory of how it had once felt to hold those in his palm.

How she was still the most beautiful woman he'd ever seen was beyond him. He had spent *years* living in Paris, and had counted models as some of his companions. Was it because now he knew she was pregnant? Was he imagining the glow about her, or was that simply the heat of her anger? Did it really matter?

Certainly not now that she was carrying his child. Which brought him right back to the matter at hand. He'd checked his diary before messaging his assistant. And even if it hadn't been clear, he would have made it so.

'Will this weekend suffice?' he asked her, knowing that it would throw her. Knowing that it would confuse her. A small, mean part of him relished the fact that she might feel just a little of what he was currently struggling with.

'For what?'

'Our wedding.'

'Wedding? I can't marry you!' she cried, throwing her hands up in the air. 'What on earth would the family think? That I'm so desperate to get my hands on Gallo Group that I'd sell myself by marrying—'

Her words halted dramatically mid-sentence and mid-air, the temperature in the room dropping to freezing from his anger.

'What were you going to say, *cara*?' he demanded. 'That you were prostituting yourself? To someone like me? The illegitimate bastard son of a whore who inherited everything they'd always wanted?'

'Micha, I—'

But he didn't want to hear it. Didn't want her to take back her unthinking words. Because he needed to know, needed to remember what she thought about him. He couldn't go into this blindly and naively like he had before.

'I've been called worse. I don't care what they think,' he dismissed.

'But *I* do,' she said, her eyes bright with indignation.

'And that's always been your problem, Maria. One that I'm more than happy to exploit to my advantage.'

'What do you mean?' she asked.

'All I have to do is wait, Maria. Because it won't be

long until you start to show. And what do you think will happen when news of an unwed Gallo heir gets out? No, I know you better than that. So I know you'd rather marry me than drag Gallo Group through the mud by such a scandal. You might not work there any more, but you're a Gallo. You wouldn't do anything to harm the company.'

'You bastard,' she bit out.

'Yes. That is quite literally true,' he admitted. 'Which is why when I say that we will be marrying this weekend, I mean it. So let me be very clear, *bella*. There is literally *nothing* I won't do in order to ensure that my child grows up legitimate. Nothing.'

She saw it. The absolute, uncompromising truth in his gaze. When he got like this, he was a force to be reckoned with, undeniable and unstoppable. It was both absolutely pig-headed and infuriating, but once it had also been incredible.

He took a step closer to her, enough so that Maria could smell the seductive hints of his aftershave and see the hard gold glittering in his eyes.

'I would become a hound of hell myself, *cara*, if it was necessary,' he vowed, and she believed him.

Tears pressed at the backs of her eyes, but she would not, could not, let them fall. Not in front of him. What she did behind closed doors was her business, but she couldn't show this man a single hint of her vulnerability.

He was right. She *did* care what her family thought. She did care how news of her pregnancy would shake the very foundations of Gallo Group—a company that prided itself on traditional family values. A family that prided itself on them, even though not a single one of Gio's children had ever entered into a happy, successful marriage.

But she also cared that at one point in her life he was the only man she thought she might be able to have this future with: a child, a husband. He had always been the shadowy face in her fantasies. But the hatred, the anger that she saw in his gaze right now? Oh god, it was the nightmare that had come from a beautiful daydream. But she couldn't dwell on that right now.

'So other than your ego, is there a single reason that you can provide that would stop us from getting married? Stop me from providing the kind of security that *our child* would need?' he asked.

'I have my own money, Micha,' she reminded him.

It devastated her, the way he made it sound as if it were nothing but selfishness to refuse his proposal—and what proposal? *Demand* more like.

But she didn't want her child to grow up the way that he had, with the scars that he had. Oh, he might hide them well these days, but once he'd been vulnerable enough for her to catch a glimpse of them. He'd never once blamed his mother, never once treated her with anything but the respect she deserved. But Maria knew those scars were there. And she'd do anything to protect her child from those same wounds.

'This weekend?' Maria asked, hating the weakness in her voice.

'What would you gain by waiting?'

She opened her mouth, but he pressed on, regardless.

'You've already had two months. And what has that brought you? Other than a house in the middle of nowhere?' he remarked, looking around him as if the place that she had hoped would be her salvation, her sanctuary, was lacking in some way.

She wanted to argue. She wanted to rail against him, against his accusations. She wanted to pound her fists against that powerful, broad chest of his. And he looked at her as if he knew it. As if he could so easily read her every desire. Just like he had looked at her the night she'd visited him in Paris.

'Mmm?' he prodded, as if he were actually waiting for an answer.

It had brought her nothing but the mirage of time. She'd not gotten anywhere other than where she'd been when she first arrived. She'd barely even been able to unpack. As if she too knew that she wouldn't be here long.

Because in truth, she'd always known. She'd go back to him. She'd go back to him because no matter what she felt, she couldn't, *wouldn't*, keep his child from him, nor keep her child from its father. Because no matter what passed between them, she knew that he would expend his last breath making sure that his child had whatever it needed.

And that was a man she'd marry.

As if sensing her surrender, he pulled his hands out of his pockets and rocked back on his heels.

'Registry office,' she bargained.

'No.'

'What?' her head snapped up.

'No; it's a one-syllable, very common word,' he defined unnecessarily.

'Micha.'

'If you think that you will start your life as my bride, come into my home as my wife, if you think you're going to stand by my side at the very least until our child is of legal, adult age, having had some secret, out-of-the-way wedding with no photos or family as if we are *ashamed*, then you are very wrong.'

She flinched, seeing it how he'd seen it and regretting her request instantly. 'I didn't mean it like that,' she whispered.

'Then what did you mean? Every single Gallo that has married in the last twenty years, with the exception of Antonio, has had the centre spread in *Hello Magazine*.'

'Oh, and you think you can organise that in less than four working days, do you?' she shot back, instead of answering his question.

'You would do well not to underestimate me, Maria,' he warned and she heeded.

'Nor you, me, Micha,' she said, feeling the hot scouring heat of anger crawling up her spine. She was tired of his threats, and if she was being honest, was a little bit hurt too. 'You think you can come in here and make demands that upend my life and that I have no say? What about after the wedding, huh? What about *after* you've put your ring on my finger and claimed me in front of the world?' *Like some trophy*, she mentally added. 'You'll go back to work running the company you know should be mine, while I stay at home and play wife and mother?'

'Play?' he asked, an arched eyebrow raised in a challenge.

'You know what I mean,' she dismissed.

'No, I don't,' he said, leaning back from the breakfast bar. 'The Maria I knew would never have kept such a secret to herself.'

'The Maria you knew grew up after you left,' she shot back, wishing his gaze wasn't so unfathomable. 'She stopped making assumptions long ago, so yes. Before I even consider agreeing to your proposal, I want to know what marriage looks like to you.'

She saw the muscle flex in his jaw, knew that his silence was not mutinous, nor malicious. He was struggling to formulate his words in that way that he sometimes did when his emotions became too much. The realisation, a knowing left over from a time when they had been close, when she had thought that perhaps they loved each other, hit her hard and took her own frantic pulse rate down a little. Because this wasn't easy for him. And somehow that made it less painful for her.

'I will not have our child growing up like you—watching your mother stand in silence while her husband flaunts his affairs for all and sundry,' he announced, the verbal blow striking a bullseye. It had been that silence, that mute acceptance of the most awful carelessness that had driven Maria almost entirely through her life, determined never to be that person, never to let another person turn her into a *statue*, with no other purpose than to stand there and look pretty.

'Nor shall it grow up like me,' he continued, cutting into her thoughts, and stopping himself before he could describe a childhood that she already knew. It had never been a secret that his mother had been forced to sell herself on the streets after his father abandoned them the day Micha was born. Perhaps, she thought for the first time, it should have been. Perhaps his shame would have been easier to bear—not that she believed for even a second that he *should* have been ashamed.

How on earth were they—two broken people—supposed to raise something so pure, so innocent and so utterly dependent on them? When they hated each other.

But you don't. You don't hate him.

She pushed her inner voice down where she couldn't hear it any more.

'What did you mean about my mother?' she asked, wanting to know, needing him to be clear.

He frowned, the slash of his brow dark over his eyes.

'Affairs?' she forced herself to ask.

It was clear that Micha wanted a traditional marriage, but…

'There will be no affairs, Maria.'

His words reverberated in the room with his vehemence.

'I—'

'So that there is no confusion, after our marriage you, and our child, will come to live with me. We will live together until our child is eighteen. We will appear united and very much in love to every single person that knows us. Family, colleagues, the journalists that swarm this family like wasps, even the parents of our child's friends. The entire world will envy our marriage, Maria. So there will be no affairs. And before you can rage in accusation that I would have any different role in this marriage, I will never share my bed with another woman while my ring is on your finger.'

Maria scoffed.

'I'm not a savage, Maria. I can control myself.'

'For eighteen years?'

'Yes.'

There was no compromise in his response. No room for her to question or doubt. He meant every word he said.

Her phone on the countertop vibrated, causing it to jump a little across the smooth marble.

And yet Micha didn't take his eyes off her.

The phone continued to ring, completely ignorant of the battle of wills that was happening around it.

This marriage? This *kind* of marriage? It was everything she'd never wanted for herself. Everything she'd spent her entire life trying to avoid. But for her child? For the security, the legitimacy, the protection, he could offer them? There wasn't even a single moment's hesitation.

She nodded in agreement.

'Okay,' he said, his gaze flicking across to her phone. He picked it up and swiped the screen to accept the call, as if he had the damn right.

'Ivy? What are you and your husband doing on Saturday?' he asked and just like that, Maria's life changed *again*.

CHAPTER SIX

You need to get down here right now.

MICHA LOOKED AT the message Ivy Gallo had sent him less than ten minutes ago and checked the location share on the map. He was less than fifty metres away from the shop they were in, but he forced himself to stop. To breathe. To *think*.

It had been four days since he had left Maria's rented cottage near Lake Trasimeno and with only two days before the wedding he still hadn't wrapped his head around *her*. His assistant had kept him updated on her movements, Maria seeming to prefer to communicate with Eduardo rather than him—something he was both thankful and slightly resentful over.

Eduardo had informed him that Maria had checked into the hotel La Tormalina last night but her belongings and personal effects were still at the lake house. It wasn't that he'd expected her to magically uproot her life and integrate it into his, he told himself. That would be an outrageous assumption for anyone to make, he recognised, even as the twist of dissatisfaction tightened in his gut.

But he couldn't help but feel that it was symbolic of her holding back. Of her not realising the situation that she was in. They were in. He wouldn't, couldn't accept half measures in this. He'd been young when he learned that lesson and he'd learned it hard. But it was a lesson that had dragged him from the streets to the dizzying heights of control of one of the world's largest conglomerates.

At seven years old, he'd not had the luxury of time to adjust. He'd known that if he hadn't acted immediately, the next man his mother sold herself to might just kill her. That was the day he'd met Gio Gallo and his life had changed. It wasn't luck. It was because Micha had made a decision. It was because he had decided to go all in that Micha had picked the richest mark, the person he could steal the most from. And honestly, for a moment there he'd thought he'd got away with it. But Gio had been too clever for him. The Italian businessman had let him escape, but only so far. Micha hadn't even imagined that the man had followed him all the way back to where he lived.

And while it wasn't in the way he'd expected, Micha's life *had* changed that day. Gio had plucked him and his mother from the slums they'd barely been able to afford, and given them housing, given Micha an education, given first his mother work and then, when he'd been old enough, Micha had worked for Gio too; whatever the older man said, whatever he wanted, Micha made it happen.

And in just two days' time it would change again.

When Maria became his wife.

Micha followed the location arrow on the map on the screen of his cellphone until he was right on top of it. Looking up at the boutique Ivy had brought him to, he winced. Mentally cursing, he blew out a reluctant breath of air and braced himself.

The bell chimed as he crossed the threshold, but no

one rushed to greet him and he soon discovered why as he ventured further into the bridal store.

'Absolutely not.'

The sounds of a somewhat heated argument came from somewhere in the back, he guessed, because he couldn't see past the rows and rows of dresses in various shades of white and increasing states of bouffant.

'But Ms Gallo, the designer assured me—'

'As the designer isn't here, I'm having considerable trouble wondering how on earth she could have assured you that I look anything other than absolutely hideous!' he heard Maria insist.

If the shop assistant knew what was good for her, she should probably give up the argument. Maria had never been one to back down from a fight, ever.

And just like that, a childhood memory flashed into his mind. About two years after Gio had 'adopted' him, in an attempt to civilise the hellion that he'd been, Micha had been sent to the same school as Antonio and Maria. They'd been inseparable back then. Not that it had stopped some opportunistic kids trying to bully him. The day he'd been about to prove exactly why it was futile to do so, Maria—half a head smaller than both him and the wannabe bully—pushed her way in between them and threated what amounted to grievous bodily harm if the kid didn't stop.

He rubbed his jaw, fighting the smile that threated to crack across his features from the memory.

'The style of dress perhaps—' the shop assistant pressed on, heedless of Maria's ire.

'Is terrible? Awful? Makes me look like my grandmother? Ivy, you can see it, can't you?'

'Well…'

'Oh, you're so *English*, Ivy. Too polite to say anything negative,' Maria dismissed as Micha drew closer to the dressing area. Between peach-coloured draped silk, he caught glimpses of a raised dais, and several mirrors.

The assistant was helping Maria out of something puffy and white as Ivy turned, her eyes widening to see him, both in relief and warning.

Few knew that he and Ivy had met several years ago when Gio Gallo had sent him to try to bribe her into divorcing Antonio, thereby leaving Antonio free to marry Maria as Gio intended. Ivy had earned both his and Gio's respect when she had turned down a life-changing amount of money, instead choosing to stand beside the husband of a convenient marriage that soon proved to be so much more. And that respect had developed into like, forging a strange unspoken understanding and respect between him and Ivy. In some ways, Micha felt that she had seen him in a light that Antonio and Maria would never, because she wasn't tarnished by the Gallo family prejudice.

'Help,' Ivy mouthed and he couldn't stop the smile that came to his lips—the moment of humour easing something of the stress and tension that had held him taut for the last four days.

'It's not funny!' she mouthed again and he bit his lip to stop the laughter in his chest.

It wasn't. It really wasn't. But there was something painfully familiar about Maria's frustration over something as simple as a wedding dress.

Behind Ivy, the assistant had manoeuvred Maria into another bright white dress that made him wince. The low-cut neckline created more cleavage than he'd even thought possible for Maria, then puffed out beneath her breasts in a way that reminded him of a Victorian milk maid, creating an uncomfortable discord between the competing images of purity and impropriety. The shocking bright white made Maria look almost sick in the harsh lighting and he wasn't in the least surprised when Maria fisted her hands at her sides and let out a cry of frustration.

Which was nothing compared to the cry of alarm she made when she caught sight of him standing there.

Maria's heart dropped to the floor the moment she caught Micha standing on the brink of the dressing area.

Oh god, what was he doing here?

'You're not supposed to see me in my wedding dress!' she cried pulling her arms around her waist as if she could protect herself from his gaze.

She *hated* that he was seeing her like this. *Hated* that he was seeing her look so *hideous*.

Especially when he looked... She scrunched her eyes together, but the image of him standing there in that damn near perfect suit made him look like a model, harsh cheekbones, broad shouldered, thin hipped and that waistcoat that she remembered far too well.

'Don't worry about bad luck, *cara*, because there is no way that you'll be marrying me wearing *that*,' he assured her.

And she hated that she agreed with him too. At least, she thought, slowly prising her eyes open, he wasn't planning to punish her by forcing her to wear something as hideous as this in two days' time.

Two days.

We have very little time for alterations, Ms Gallo, so

we will need to find something that fits as close to your size as possible.

Maria knew that. And she intensely disliked being difficult, she would *never* normally be so demanding. But this was important. It was her wedding dress. And while it might not be the day she'd ever imagined for herself, it was *vital* that her dress be perfect.

Because of what *they* would say, what *they* would think.

Her parents. Her family. The Gallos.

Clothes were armour. And she needed armour. She needed to be as protected as possible when she stood before every single member of the Gallo family and married Micha. Because no matter how many times she had proved herself worthy, had worked harder than any other family member, longer than any other employee, gone above and far beyond whatever anyone else had ever done at Gallo Group, it had never been enough.

Not for her grandfather, who deemed her inferior because of her gender, *unworthy* of inheriting a company she could run better than anyone. Not for her parents, who had shown her nothing but irritation and disappointment for not being their much-needed *male* heir; the only way they thought they could have pleased Gio Gallo. And not Micha, who had left the first chance he could get.

Oh, she could hear the snide whispers and barely concealed critiques.

Pregnant. Desperate. Coerced.

Or worse.

That she'd got her hands on Gallo Group the only way she'd ever be capable of getting it, by trapping Micha with a pregnancy. Because she 'wasn't good enough' to earn it. But she *had* been. She'd been better than all of them. Even Micha. But in the end none of that would matter, because now they'd all think that she'd manipulated all this to get what she didn't deserve.

'Could you give us a moment?' Micha asked both the assistant and Ivy.

Ivy shot her a glance in the mirror and Maria nodded, not wanting to argue the point—certain that she didn't want Ivy to hear what Micha was about to say. Maria waited, breath locked in her lungs until they were alone.

She felt...vulnerable, exposed and she didn't like it.

'What did you tell her?' he asked as he started pacing the dais in a slow circle.

'Ivy? You mean, after you invited her to a wedding on the day that she knew you'd discovered that I was pregnant? I don't think even the most gullible would have believed that it was true love, Micha.'

He sighed, impatient with her answer.

'I told her that you were ridiculously happy. That it was the best news you'd ever heard,' she said, her angry whisper the opposite of her words. 'I told her that you confessed that you'd always loved me, ever since...' And she couldn't do it. Couldn't bring herself to touch on the precious, tender, painful past they shared. 'And that... you'd only ever imagined a future with me in it and...that you wanted to marry me and make me and our child happy.' Her explanation stuttered out past hurts and long-forgotten dreams and heartache that felt fresh even to this day. *God*, how she wished the story she'd spun around their betrothal was true. Tears pressed against the backs of her eyes and she turned away, biting her lip until the sting of pain pushed back the emotional rollercoaster her pregnancy had pushed her into.

'Va bene.'

She closed her eyes, hoping to compose herself, pressing a hand against the tight neckline that was making it hard for her to breathe.

'Take that off. It's making me uncomfortable,' he ordered.

She scoffed. 'Making *you* uncomfortable? *You* don't have to wear it.'

'Neither do you,' he pointed out with infuriating rationality. 'So, take it off.'

'I *can't*. You sent away the assistant,' she threw at him accusingly.

He glared at her before closing the distance between them in long, powerful strides. She watched him in the reflection of the mirror as he came behind her on the raised dais, gently kicking the wide expanse of the skirts out of the way so that he could get close enough to where the zip was concealed by a row of one hundred satin-covered buttons.

She felt the heat of him across the bare skin of her shoulder blades, inhaled the scent of leather and spice, something *tempting*. Her heart pounded against her ribcage, her body craving his expert touch, aflame with need that whipped up like an unexpected tornado that touched down over them, keeping them in the eye of a storm that had not exhausted itself three months ago.

He stared down at the zip that would set her free. Breath caught in her lungs, pressing her chest deeper against the neckline that was so confining. And for a heartbeat his gaze flickered between her back and her

chest in the mirror in front of her and she wanted to…
She wanted to…

Surrender.

She was a madness in his blood. How could it be that he had not satiated his desire already? How could it be that even as he fought and railed against what he'd been forced to do—what he'd forced her into, marriage—that *still* he wanted her? Self-recrimination was powerful, harsh and swift.

He found the tab at the top of the zip and yanked it free, stepping away from the dais before he could do what he really wanted to do. Which was rip the dress from her body and take her like the animal he truly was beneath all outward signs of sophistication.

He gritted his teeth and shoved his fisted hands into his pockets as he focused solely on the dresses around him—anything other than where Maria was navigating her way out of that monstrosity and into a satin dressing gown that did nothing to hide the perfection of her body.

Cazzo.

But damn, it was better than the look in her eyes just before…the glistening of her eyes, the tremble of the lip she'd tried to hide from him. He hated that she did that, kept what she was feeling from him. But he understood it. After all, couldn't he say the same?

They didn't trust each other. How could they? But they would need to. If they were going to get through this, they would have to do it together.

'Why did you let her put you in that thing?' he asked, genuinely curious and a little surprised that she *had* let the assistant put her in that dress.

There was a moment's hesitation.

'She is trying to make me look...slimmer.'

Slimmer? He opened his mouth to object, until he realised what she was saying. She was trying to hide her pregnancy. Their pregnancy.

'Are you ashamed?' he asked, spinning round to confront her, struggling with the anger that was so quick to ignite. He couldn't, wouldn't, allow her to be ashamed of their child...of *him*.

He saw the clench of her teeth, the little flutter of the muscle at her jaw, the way her body straightened as if ready to fight, *always* ready to fight.

'I am not, and never will be, ashamed of my child,' she said with a blaze of glory that made him both proud and instantly relieved. 'And I will do everything in my power to protect our child from whatever snide comments and meanness comes their way, from whatever quarter; family, friend or foe. But,' she said, her shoulders threatening to slump, 'I would just like to avoid, if possible, any nasty speculation on our wedding day.'

And when she turned her back to him to reach for a glass of water, he remembered how much she'd always dreamed of a huge white wedding, a church full of her friends and family, of the perfect dress. He saw how that in some small way she was trying to keep hold of that fantasy. And he understood that. He knew how mean the Gallos could be. They were like a pack of hyenas when they got it in their minds. But she was one of them. And she had chosen them.

She will always choose them.

Gio's voice echoed in his mind as he scanned the rails of dresses that lined the walls of the dressing area.

A cream silk confection caught his eye and he pulled the sleek-lined dress from the rack. Further down was another—a gently corseted dress with a sweetheart neckline, and one last one that was the complete opposite of either: lace detailed over the lightest gauze, with tiny little sparkling diamonds.

Just behind it, though, was a dress that stopped him in his tracks. The neckline dropped in a sweeping V into a wide belted waist, long draped material fell from slightly puffed shoulder sleeves into cuffs at the wrist and the skirt fell away in a swathe of oyster silk. It was soft, romantic, all the things Maria rejected, but had never managed to fully hide about herself. It was the dress he'd have chosen for her eleven years ago. But they weren't seventeen. Not any more. And too much had passed between then and now for them to go back.

Instead, he reached for the dress with the sparkling diamonds and placed all three on the back of an empty chair.

'One of these will do,' he said, forcing a boredom into his voice he knew she would view as a challenge. Far better for her to be angry than upset.

He checked his watch, trying to ignore the way a delicate blush pinked her cheeks.

'I have to go. You will be okay?'

'I was perfectly okay before you got here,' she growled like an angry kitten and he tried not to smile.

'You were about to let a woman convince you to wear a dress that made you look like a pornographic milk maid. You were *not* okay.'

'Get out!'

This time he couldn't hold it back. The laugh fell from his lips like sand slipping through his fingers, unstoppable and horrifyingly easy. It wasn't mean, there was nothing nasty in it, nothing tainted the air between them and he wasn't completely sure but he thought he saw her smile, a glitter in her eyes that wasn't sad, or hurt. But then the laughter quietened, leaving a silence between them that wasn't hot like it had been in Paris, or hurt like it had been earlier that week. It was something that was too close to what they'd had *before*.

He nodded once, to himself, as if putting a full stop on the exchange.

'I'll see you tomorrow night.'

'Tomorrow night?' she asked.

'*Si*, did you not check your emails? We have the rehearsal dinner.'

The pretty blush on her cheeks paled, leaving her looking wan under the harsh lighting. 'We *can't*,' she said, and just like that, they were back to where they always were. At loggerheads, with her ashamed to be with him and him never being good enough for her.

'We can and we will, *cara*,' he decreed, before turning on his heel and cursing whatever foolishness had made him think, even for a second, otherwise.

Maria watched him leave, wishing that they could have held onto that moment just a little bit longer. That brief reprieve from the constant anger and resentment that simmered between them. But it was hopeless. Too much time had gone, too much hurt. Gio had chosen Micha, Micha had chosen him and the only person Maria could choose was herself.

Then and now.

She looked over to the rack that Micha had chosen the

three dresses from and, unable to help herself, crossed the room. One by one, she flicked through the dresses, hoping to find what had caught his eye—the dress he'd *not* chosen for her. She frowned as she passed glittering sparkles and lace, not thinking it would have been one of those until…

There. It was beautiful. Simple lines, the low V suiting her chest size, the soft, loose, but utterly elegant drapes of silk were romantic and would hide the small thickening of her waist without constriction.

'Oh, that's perfect!' Ivy cried from behind her. 'You must try it on,' she insisted.

Maria bit her lip and swallowed. 'No, I don't think so,' she replied, instinctively knowing that it *was* perfect and that she *should* try it on. But if he'd wanted to see her in it…

And since when did you start doing whatever the men in your life wanted you to do?

Since they won, Maria mentally replied.

She settled the dresses back on the rack, hoping that the dress would get lost in among the others, but knowing that she'd find it again in a heartbeat if she wanted to.

She shook herself out of the melancholy of the moment and turned to Ivy with a smile.

'The groom himself chose three dresses for me, so I suppose I should give those a go first, yes?'

Ivy nodded, but the concern was still bright in the light blue eyes that stared back at Maria. Forcing a little more effort into her smile, she rubbed Ivy's arm in reassurance and returned to the dais with one of the dresses Micha had chosen.

'You know that you don't have to do this if you don't

want to,' Ivy said, her eyes firmly fixed on Maria, who concentrated on getting herself into the corseted dress with the sweetheart neckline.

Where was the assistant?

'Maria?'

The zip was nearly impossible to undo and she hadn't even got herself into it yet. Her fingers struggled with the tiny little piece of plastic, but everything was just so blurry she couldn't see. She wiped her eye with the back of her hand and was surprised when it came back wet.

'Maria,' Ivy said, much closer to her this time, putting her hands over where Maria's fingers clutched the zip. Ivy gently pushed the dress away and wrapped her arms around her tightly, as Maria's breath shuddered in her lungs. So slowly, so slightly, Maria felt herself gently rocked and soothed by her cousin's wife.

'Let's run away,' Ivy whispered into her ear, and Maria let out a bark of miserable laughter. 'Just you and me. Antonio will catch us up. Micha will never find us. You know what Antonio is like when he puts his mind to something. We'll all live together, and raise our children and have nothing but blue skies, laughter and all the love we need.'

Maria didn't think her heart could take the idyllic picture that a woman who had quickly become like a sister to her had painted. She wanted it so badly. But she knew she couldn't do it. Couldn't have it. Because when she imagined it, Micha was there. Not scowling or angry, or bitter. But smiling and happy and... That was nothing but a fantasy.

'Let me do this for you. Let me kidnap you,' Ivy begged. That the English librarian who was so very different from Maria would do that for her warmed some of the hurt and filled some of the fractures in her heart. She knew that Ivy felt guilty, that she and Antonio had fallen in love with each other. And that if they hadn't, then Antonio would have married her—as directed by Gio Gallo's last will and testament—and they would have inherited Gallo Group, and Antonio would have given it over to her entirely, having no personal or professional interest in running it himself.

'*Grazie*, Ivy. I believe you'd do it too,' Maria laughed sadly.

'I would,' she replied fiercely. 'You're not alone, Maria. You will never be alone again.'

But Maria thought that Ivy was wrong. It was clear that Ivy didn't realise that sometimes you could be lonelier in a marriage than you could ever be outside of one. And it was devastating to Maria to realise that despite all her intentions to avoid being like her parents—like her mother—she had ended up in exactly the same position.

Only, unlike her mother, Maria thought as she swept a hand over her abdomen, she wouldn't allow her child to become caught in the crossfire of such emotional neglect. She would do better, *be* better. She would, Maria realised, fight everyone and everything to ensure that her child grew up never feeling the sting of being deemed unworthy or inferior for any reason.

But that had to start with her, first. She had to find her armour again, she realised as she looked back to the rack of dresses.

'You're coming to the rehearsal dinner?' she asked Ivy as she swept the dress on the floor aside with her foot.

'Yes,' Ivy replied, unfazed by the sudden direction change of their conversation.

'Good. Where is the shop assistant?'

'Here, Signora Gallo,' the harried young woman replied rushing back into the changing room.

'I'm going to need a suit.'

'A suit?' the woman blinked.

'*Si*. A three-piece suit. In white,' Maria replied, unaware of the fierce glint, and sudden glow that made her features come alive.

CHAPTER SEVEN

MICHA REFUSED TO check his watch. He knew what the time was and Maria wasn't late. Not yet anyway. But unease swirled around him, making his body feel uncomfortable, his clothes feel too tight. The foyer of the central Rome hotel glistened elegantly in soft cream lighting, perfect to highlight the rich buttery marble flooring veined in black. But tension corded his shoulder muscles and he rolled his head to ease the ache, righting it before a couple entered from the bar area and caught sight of such weakness.

There could be none. Not tonight.

The entire Gallo clan had shown up. He wasn't surprised, but he was impressed. Whether it was their curiosity or their avarice that drove them, every single one of them wanted to see the new head of the Gallo Group and his fiancée, as if they were some spectator sport.

He hated it as much as he needed it, because he hadn't lied to Maria. He hadn't been exaggerating when he'd told her that everyone would believe in the veracity of this marriage. His child would grow up with nothing less.

Which was why he was doing this properly, the rehearsal dinner. Her family. His mother. Even now, his mother was sitting among them, and he didn't trust a single Gallo up there not to treat her the way she deserved to be treated: with respect, with honour.

He knew how they had seen him, let alone her. But not a single one of them knew what it was like to be desperate. To be so determined to put food in your child's belly that you'd sell yourself and your soul to do it.

Micha slowly and carefully uncurled the fist his hand had formed and smoothed his palm down the waistcoat of his black suit, pulling himself together. His mother had assured him that she would be fine, and he knew she would be. Rosa Rufina was made of stronger stuff than the Gallos could even imagine.

The old-fashioned circular doorway to the hotel began to move and he knew. He knew that she had arrived. He could feel it on his skin, in the way that his breath hitched and his heart pulled. He'd thought he was over that kind of stuff, but when Maria emerged into the foyer, he knew it had been nothing but a lie.

She was glorious.

Rich waves of espresso-coloured hair tumbled around her bare shoulders. The cream waistcoat dipped low, but not salaciously so, and perfectly matched the pressed wide-leg trousers. Her lips, a shocking slash of bright crimson, were a carnal focal point to an appearance that was expensive, confident, professional, powerful. All the things that he'd always admired about her.

And if he thought about the look of vulnerability that he'd seen in the bridal shop the day before, then he pushed that out of his mind as she closed the distance between them.

The click of her cream heels counted down the seconds until she joined him and when she did, she gave him a slow perusal from head to toe. Her blank response, presumably supposed to irritate him, only amused him. He knew what he looked like—he was neither arrogant, nor egotistical. And he knew—the memory of that night in Paris coming to him in a flash—that she liked the way he looked.

'Did anyone cancel?' she asked.

It was the first thing out of her mouth. Not *Hello, how are you?* She wanted to know if anyone had the audacity to snub his demand that they attend this rehearsal dinner. She was probably calculating the impact on the stock prices if anyone had the temerity to do so.

Her nod of acknowledgement was only momentarily hesitant, betraying her surprise. He frowned, thrown by the 'tell'. She had clearly thought that a member of her family would refuse to come. Did she have someone particular in mind, or—

His chain of thought was cut off when she angled her head up to his and he fell into large brown eyes, wide and so dark as to be unfathomable. It was as if he were underwater, holding his breath—lost to this moment that he wanted to stay in—but starved for oxygen and sanity, he returned to reality, and held out his arm for her to take.

Together, they made their way up the grand red-carpeted spiral staircase to where the hotel had converted a ballroom into one of Rome's most sought-after restaurants. But instead of being led to a table there, the maître d' gestured for them to follow him round to the private room that Micha had secured for the rehearsal dinner.

Maria's eyes flicked to his, probably mentally calculating the amount of money that this would set him back. Again, always underestimating him, just like every other

Gallo, and he stifled the spark of irritation that sprang to life.

Beyond the closed doors, the loud sound of voices pressed up against the wood.

Micha went to raise his hand to push them open, but stopped when Maria's fingers gripped his jacket sleeve.

'What is it?' he asked, as he noticed the tension in her body, the slight tightening around her lips.

'A united front, right? No matter what happens, no matter what…is *said*.'

'Maria—'

She shook her head to cut off his question and removed her hand from his arm, visibly gathering herself. And he couldn't quite work it out. This was her family. They were her people. The ones she had chosen over him, and probably would again, given half the chance. Stage fright. That's all it must have been, he thought as he pushed through the wooden doors, the raised voices of moments ago falling away into complete silence.

Maria's heart pounded in her ears. She hadn't realised that she would be so…*scared*. Instinctively her gaze sought out Antonio and Ivy, her lifelines this evening, and a warm breath shivered through her as she saw Ivy's obvious encouragement and Antonio's clear and slightly murderous glare at Micha. It was enough to soften the edges of the tension around her body and allowed her the first smile she'd had since she and Ivy had left the bridal shop the day before.

As for the rest of the room, a total of thirty-five Gallos were seated at a banquetstyle table and she doubted the place settings had been an accident. Her distant cousins and aunts and uncles—related to Gio through his siblings—were at the far end of the table. Closer to the head was Alessina Gallo, Antonio's mother and Gio's eldest, sitting beside the middle brother, Maria's Uncle Carlos. Their younger sister, who had been disowned by their father years before, was still only slowly making her way back into the family fold and had, according to Micha, politely declined. Her son Enzo and wife were also away, but would be there tomorrow. Her eyes rested on Rosa Rufina, the woman sitting at the left of the two seats at the head of the table where she and Micha would sit, and smiled.

It was instinctive. Maria hadn't seen Rosa for years, the realisation hitting her with something like guilt. Gio had moved both Micha and Rosa to Paris, and Maria had been so consumed with her own feelings that she had forgotten the woman who had always treated her with a gentle, reserved kindness. It was still there in the older woman's gaze when she met Maria's, a small smile gracing her lips, but an understanding shining in her eyes that Maria didn't think she'd get from her own family.

And then she looked to the couple that sat opposite Rosa. Her parents.

Her father refused to meet her gaze in what could only be the most obvious and blatant snub. The clenched jaw, the simmering anger—he'd have done better not to bother turning up. The shame of his disappointment burned her cheeks and her heart. Her mother's eyes flickered to hers and then back to her plate, her apathy more painful than her father's rejection.

Her fingers dug into the superfine black wool jacket over Micha's forearms, sacrificing all the hard work she'd done to put on her armour. It was nothing but a mirage.

White knuckles would have betrayed her, and she was about to withdraw when his large hand covered hers. She wasn't entirely sure that he'd done it on purpose, but for a single breath his surprising act of kindness struck her dumb.

'Thank you all for coming,' Micha announced as he ushered her into the seat at the head of the table, before kissing his mother on the cheek and nodding at her father as if he wasn't being so painfully and obviously rude.

As waiters came round and filled glasses, Micha welcomed her family on behalf of him and his mother. Proclaiming how happy he was that Maria and he had found each other. That he couldn't have ever imagined another woman by his side and that tomorrow she would finally make him an honest man.

She flinched when someone down the far end had the audacity to scoff out loud.

He ignored it all. Instead, he was charming, not overly so, and witty; perfectly pitched. Maria had never seen him handle her family because his role had kept him primarily in Paris. She'd never really thought about how he would manage them, because she'd been so angry and so hurt that she'd refused to consider that he might actually be able to. But also because until now, the only person who had been able to wrangle the Gallos had been her grandfather.

God, she missed him. It was a strange thing. He might have never considered her truly worthy in her own right to take over Gallo Group, but he had still encouraged her, given her a role in the family business that made use of the skills other family members refused to acknowledge or credit her with. Yes, there was resentment there that she wasn't good enough for him, but he had been clear about it, whereas everyone else pretended and smiled while ready to stab her in the back.

As the first course was served, she watched Micha as he interacted with her family, ignoring the obvious stares and open curiosity around the table. She wanted to speak to Antonio and Ivy, she wanted to be anywhere else than here, but she was trapped by her parents' stony silence.

At some point her father got up from the table without even bothering to excuse himself. It was only when he didn't come back that Maria began to notice—along with several other members of the family.

Clenching her jaw, she excused herself.

In the quiet of the hallway outside the private dining room, she finally found the space to breathe. She hadn't realised how oppressive the sounds of the entire clan had been. Prising her eyes back open, she looked around for her father.

She heard him before she saw him.

'Yes, you needed to know... No, I want to continue our good relationship and thought you would be interested in who you are doing business with... Well, after, things will continue as they were.'

Business? Her father was talking business? Now?

'Papa,' she said as she rounded the corner, to find him ending the call and slipping his mobile phone into his pocket.

He looked at her with such disdain that she flinched, but she wasn't ready to back down. Not yet.

'It's my rehearsal dinner, Papa,' she pleaded.

'Rehearsal dinner? Isn't it a little too late for that?' he said, his gaze narrowing on her stomach. 'You should have kept your legs closed. You had one job, one!' he yelled, not bothering to keep his voice down. 'You were supposed to marry *well*. And instead you lay with that stray dog, Rufina.'

He might as well have slapped her. Her mouth fell open and she took a step back.

'We'll never be free of that bastard now. *Never*. And if you think for one moment that I'll be paying for this farce of a wedding—'

'That won't be necessary, Luca.'

Maria froze at the sound of Micha's voice from behind her.

Facing him, she saw the moment of shock in her father's eyes, and watched it turn to anger and defiance.

'I meant what I said,' her father snarled.

'So did I,' Micha responded. 'You won't be paying for a single part of this wedding.'

Micha took a step closer, enough to feel the warmth rising from Maria's body, the fluttering of her pulse at her jaw, from where she turned her head ever so slightly, to hear him berate her father.

'Luca, let me be very clear. I will never allow you to drip your poison into my family ever again. You may be present, you may observe, but you will never speak to Maria again unless she wishes it. You will not contact her, unless she wishes it. As for our child? Again, any contact will be on Maria's terms.'

'Or what, Rufina?'

'Luca, I will sever Gallo Group in half if I must just to get rid of you.'

'You wouldn't dare,' Luca said, stepping back in shock.

'Try me. I've gone head to head with your father. And trust me, you are not him.'

Maria's shocked inhale echoed between them, as Micha stared into the eyes of his future father-in-law. Oh, he wasn't naive. He knew that Maria's father would want to retaliate. He may even try. But Micha learned a long time ago that there was only one way to deal with a spoilt, talentless, insecure Gallo like Luca. And that was to knock him down hard and fast.

Luca clenched his jaw and glared back, anger reddening his cheeks unpleasantly. Eventually he pushed past his daughter and went back into the dining room.

Maria held herself taut for just a moment more before releasing her breath in a shudder.

And in that moment, he'd never hated a Gallo more. All the fight, all the defiance, the power and the determination that had pushed Maria to such dizzying heights at the Gallo Group had fled when confronted with her father's rejection. Something he understood in a way that Maria would probably never realise. Because he'd had that kind of relationship with Gio. Oh, he was their grandfather by blood, but for all of Gio's complicated and sometimes bigoted beliefs, the man had been like a father to him and he'd never wanted to let him down. Not once. And especially not when he'd been seventeen.

Hauling himself back to the present, Micha held out his arm for Maria to take, all the while wrestling with the fierce anger coursing through his veins, blocking out the sounds of spluttering outrage that Luca Gallo had left making. He led Maria back to the room where the rest of the Gallos waited, the whispers and gossip far too much for him to permit now that the lines had been drawn.

He showed Maria to her seat, and then bent to whisper to his mother that he was arranging a taxi to take her back to his home. He pulled out his phone and messaged his assistant to come and meet his mother and make the necessary arrangements. He didn't want her there for what he was about to do.

He felt Maria's questioning gaze on his, but he didn't have the time or the capacity at that precise moment to explain. All the words he wanted jumbled on his tongue, anger making him rash, and he couldn't afford to be either rash or incomprehensible.

Silence had fallen over the room as he pulled his mother's chair out for her and escorted her to the door where his assistant was already waiting. Maria's father returned to the room shortly after with a face that was both shocked and furious and Micha wanted to laugh. He hadn't seen anything yet.

He'd always known what the Gallos thought of him. He'd known that Gio had used the threat of leaving the family company to him as a whipping post for his family, a threat to keep them all in line. But they had grown even more greedy, their avarice increasing in line with the profit of Gallo Group. They were a monster, a cancer, and they had to be stopped.

It was one thing to turn on him, but to turn on her? On Maria? On one of their own?

How had Gio not stepped in to stop this kind of thing? Micha knew she'd had to work hard to get even the smallest amount of respect at Gallo Group, but this? The way that they picked on her, ignored her, treated her? Gio should have stopped it. Her father should have damn well done it, but he was the worst of them. And Antonio? What had he been doing all the time she had been treated like this? Fury bit into his soul and clung on.

He returned to the table, where, rather than taking his seat, he gripped the back of the chair and stared down the length of the table. He caught the concerned gaze that Antonio sent his fiancée's way, half rising from his chair, but Ivy pressed him back down and he felt a rush of affection for Antonio's English wife, a woman who had seemed to understand him more than the people in this room who had known him nearly his entire life. He waited until every single gaze in the room was on him, before starting.

'I understand some of you here may be under the impression that I was little more than Gio's thug,' he said with a shrug. 'I understand why, so there are no hard feelings. I also understand that it will have taken some time to acclimatise to the unexpected terms of Gio's last will and testament that installed me as the new CEO. So, I'm going to take this opportunity to clarify a few things.

'You have all grown a little too comfortable with the levels of disrespect and unprofessionalism. And that stops here. There will be no more whispers, snide comments, disparaging remarks and back stabbing. Neither professionally nor personally. Both you and Gallo Group are hovering on the brink of an abyss. If you continue down this path,' he warned, 'it is you, not me, that will lose everything. I don't care what you think of me, frankly, as long as you keep it to yourselves.

'But Maria?' he said, letting loose some of his anger into his tone. 'She is my fiancée and as of tomorrow, she will be my *wife*. And if any of you dare to treat her with anything less than the respect that she deserves as a member of your family, or mine, or professionally given the amount of revenue and work that she brought to Gallo Group—something that far outstrips the total combined income garnered by every single person at this table—then know this… You will be cut off. You will be removed from the board of governors, your shares will be dissolved and you will be banned from family events forthwith.'

Gasps of shock littered the table. Wide eyes stared back at him, and the moment the whispers started, he punched his fist into the table. The jump of cutlery and glass rippled out into surprised silence.

'And if anyone,' he pressed on, 'would like to know whether I have the authority to do this, please allow me to direct you to Alberto, the lawyer handling Gio Gallo's estate. You are welcome to try and challenge this, but I assure you, it will fail. Now, my fiancée and I have an early start in the morning, so you may all leave,' he said, gesturing to the door.

The moment that 'What?' and 'You've got to be joking' started, he punched the table again, and once again shocked the Gallos into silence.

Micha turned his attention to Luca, and locked eyes with the man who would have to leave first if any of them were going to do as commanded.

Slowly, Luca pushed his chair back from the table, seething with anger and resentment, not even bothering to spare a glance at his daughter, who had sat through Micha's pronouncement, with her gaze straight ahead—the only person who hadn't flinched when he'd struck the table. And honestly, as her father left the room, slowly followed, one after the other, by the remaining family members, he didn't know whether to be impressed or concerned by her self-possession.

Maria forced herself to uncurl her fingers as she breathed through the pounding in her chest.

He'd stood up for her.

A part of her had soared when he'd done this...but another part? Why had it made her angry? Why had it made her embarrassed? She still felt the tinge of pink on her cheeks and she tried to swallow the emotional confusion she felt now sitting at the head of an abandoned table, save for Antonio and Ivy and Micha.

Antonio threw his napkin on the table and leaned back in his chair.

'Well, that was something.'

'Yes, it was. It was something that should have been said years ago, Antonio. And not by me now,' Micha bit out.

The tension at the table shimmered in the air, Maria not quite able or willing to meet either her cousin's or Ivy's gaze.

'I didn't know it had got that bad,' Antonio admitted.
'Why didn't you tell me?' her cousin asked her.

'She shouldn't have had to!' Micha yelled.

'I was working, Micha!' Antonio yelled back. 'I was throwing everything I had into Alessina International. Where were you?'

'Gio sent me to—'

'Paris. Yeah, we know. And you can keep hiding behind that excuse all you like, Micha. But we all know that's exactly what it is. An excuse.

'Maria—' Antonio started and then stopped.

She wasn't sure why, because tears had clouded her

vision and she couldn't look up, couldn't let them see. She'd never let them see how much she'd hurt. It was a weakness. A vulnerability that they would exploit. Even now, with these people she trusted more than anyone in the entire world—even Micha—she couldn't let them see.

You were supposed to marry well.
Now we'll never be free of that bastard.
We all know that's exactly what it is. An excuse.

She was vaguely aware of Antonio and Ivy excusing themselves from the room, Ivy with a gentle brush of her hand on Maria's shoulder, and Antonio stopping to whisper something in Micha's ear. But she couldn't move. She pulled and pulled, hoping that she could hold it together, hoping that she could hold herself together, but control was slipping through her fingers. She was slipping, and sliding and hurtling towards something and she couldn't stop it.

'Let it go.'

She shook her head, even as she fought to hold on, even as tears clung to her eyelashes.

'There's no one here,' Micha said gently. 'No one will see. No one will know.'

She clenched her jaw and shook her head again. *You're here*, she wanted to say. *You'll see. You'll know.*

'You're my family now. It's okay,' he whispered and as if it were the key that she'd been waiting for her entire life, she let go.

She didn't know how long she cried for, but she came back to herself slowly, feeling more drained and wrecked than she'd ever felt before. She'd never done that. Never cried. Not like that. Not when her father failed to show up to her preschool dance recital. Not when her mother sat for dinner alone at night at a table set for two. Not when her father gave up pretence at home and moved out without bothering to say goodbye. Not even when Gio had passed. Because instead of mourning the grandfather that she had loved, despite their difficult relationship, she had been thrown into the family turmoil that bubbled and broiled at the complexities of the will.

But she had to pull herself together. She couldn't break. She couldn't do that to *her* child. Their child. She had to do better. Had to be better. As she gathered herself, she realised that she'd been in such a daze that she'd allowed Micha to do *everything*. Organise the dinner, arrange for the wedding, somehow magic up someone who had done all of this within days. And 'this' wasn't some quiet, out-of-the-way registry-office wedding. 'This' was a wedding in front of two hundred people, a priest and probably a significant number of journalists waiting outside.

It was time she did her part.

You're my family now.

Was she? She'd learned long ago that family meant different things to different people. As for what it meant to Micha, yes, he'd stood up for her tonight, but it was as much professional warning as personal. What it meant in the long run, only time would tell.

CHAPTER EIGHT

MICHA HAD NEARLY been late. For his own wedding. What a damn joke.

He'd been putting out fires that started last night. He'd expected Luca Gallo to retaliate, yes, but that quickly? He'd been surprised. Luca had a reputation as lazy, mean and selfish. It was distinctly possible that there were other family members involved, if not the whole damn lot of them. As it was, he'd only managed damage control. The rest, he'd leave for later.

For *after* the wedding.

Obviously, it had taken an obscene amount of money to gently nudge the wheels of church policy to move so quickly but as he knew the priest, knew the money would be used for good causes, Micha didn't begrudge it for one moment.

As he hastened along the ancient stone pathway to the side chapel of the church, he remembered what Antonio had said to him before leaving the restaurant last night.

She was broken after you left her. And if you do that to her again, they'll never find your body.

The threat had been laughable, but the information had near devastated him. The only way he'd got through those first few years in Paris was the white-knuckled grip he'd had on his belief that she'd have left him anyway. He couldn't have meant that much to her, because she would choose her family. A family that had never appreciated her. A family that had rejected her and still did. That's what had stung the most. That he didn't even stack up against *them*. But of course he hadn't.

He'd known at the time that Antonio would take Maria's side. He just hadn't realised that it would form a rift of resentment that even time couldn't breach.

She was broken after you left her.

Micha shook off his thoughts as he stepped into the cool, reverent interior of the church he had sneaked into when he was a child, seeking anything to assuage the ferocious summer heat. Because he'd not been able to go home. Because his father had still been there at the time, and would have given Micha a beating for sure.

And then later, after his father had left, he'd skulked in the shadows while his mother... He swallowed. There was something almost biblical about his feelings of his past and his future in that moment. Retaliation, redemption and in among it all Maria and their innocent child.

The priest's footsteps on the cool stone floor were soft.

'Micha.'

'Father.'

'It's good to see you,' Father Perosi greeted with a smile. 'Though it's been some time since your last confession.'

'I was away.'

'Mmm' was all he said in response to Micha's tenure in Paris. 'And now you are back. With a bride.'

Micha nodded, peering over his shoulder where he caught sight of filled pews.

'And in a hurry,' Father Perosi chided gently.

'Wasn't I always?'

'*Si*,' the older man said with a smile in his eyes. 'Ready?'

'Just like that? No questions about whether I'm sure, whether I'm committed?' Micha asked, only half teasing.

Father Perosi turned his considerably weighty gaze on him and Micha felt it pass beyond skin and bone until it felt as if he were gazing into Micha's very soul.

'You would not be here if you were neither sure nor committed.'

Micha nodded, knowing it as truth.

'And besides, I think you gave your heart to this woman a very long time ago.'

Micha clenched his jaw and acknowledged, reluctantly, that the priest he'd known since childhood was right. He *had* given Maria his heart a very long time ago. But she had let it go, abandoned it, *refused* it and now there was nothing but an empty space in his chest. Nothing to hope, nothing to want, nothing to hurt. Not again.

If she wasn't carrying their child, they wouldn't be here. So, while he was committed and sure about this marriage, he wasn't naive enough to think it was anything other than a way to protect their child's happiness. His happiness had never come into it.

Micha followed Father Perosi out of the small chapel into the main body of the church and towards the top of the aisle, ignoring the glares of the closest Gallos but landing on Antonio and the man beside him. Enzo Rossetti's mother—Gio's daughter—had been disowned by Gio years ago. But just before his death, Gio had reached out to Enzo and the two had become reacquainted. Micha had been only peripherally aware of the old man's attempts to meddle in the American Italian's life, as thankfully Gio had decided in this instance to do his own dirty work.

As such, Micha had only really encountered Enzo and his fiancée, Erin, a handful of times since Gio's passing. Especially since before he passed, Gio had made Enzo a member of the Gallo Group board. Undoubtedly the man was as flippant as his playboy reputation suggested, but there was something deeper there that warned Micha not to believe all that had been said about Antonio and Maria's cousin and respect the man's surprisingly good business sense.

Antonio, still clearly angry with him from the night before, glared at Micha, who turned his attention back to the proceedings.

There was no best man, and Maria had no bridesmaid. She'd have probably chosen Ivy and he wouldn't have minded, only it would have left him picking Antonio to stand behind him and while a certain amount of hostilities had subsided, given the détente reached over Micha and Ivy's surprising friendship, they were very far from the childhood friends they had once been.

Father Perosi gave him one last knowing look, and then nodded to the musical director, who managed to seamlessly blend the ongoing background music into the wedding march.

A split second before he was entirely ready, the wide wooden doors opened at the bottom of the aisle to reveal Maria standing in the open doorway and the breath left his lungs in a whoosh.

It was, he told himself later, because he had been expecting her to wear one of the dresses he'd selected in the bridal shop. Not that he was being autocratic and as much of a bastard as to insist that she should have worn one of them. It was just because he hadn't expected her to wear *that* dress.

The one that reminded him of when they'd been younger. The one that had conjured images of a future he'd told himself he'd never have. That made his pulse pound and his heart sore and soar at the same time. The one that made her look *incredible*.

Thick, dark, lazily curling hair framed her face and tumbled around her shoulders and down her back. Light touches of make-up left her natural beauty to shine all on its own, wide, large brown eyes locked on him, the plunging V neckline leading his gaze down to where she held a small bouquet of wildflowers, a miniature riot of colours that was both whimsical and fresh.

For a split second he remembered—a sunny afternoon, a feeling so powerful he thought his chest would burst, the gentle touch of fingers and lips, the warmth of sunshine from above and within, the sound of Maria's laugh and a hope for the impossible.

Then she faltered, ever so slightly, an infinitesimal pause in her stride, enough time for him only to blink and it was gone. Her hesitation, the memory, the past. It was all gone. And now a very different kind of future opened up before them. One that, he told himself, *had* to be enough.

Maria's pulse tripped and she just about managed to smooth it out without notice. She thought Micha might have caught the near wobble, but nothing had shown on his aggressively handsome face. Dark features stood out against the stark white of his dress shirt and bow tie. The light slid against the silk lapels every time Micha breathed and then got lost in the superfine black wool of his tuxedo.

High cheekbones, almost savagely sharp, and shadows beneath his eyes suggested a sleepless night. The clean shave to his jaw made him look both younger and leaner, *hungry*, *powerful*. Maria swallowed as she closed the distance between them, her gaze dropping to the sensual lips that had brought her so much pleasure. They opened then, just slightly, barely enough to draw breath, but she felt the rise of a flush on her cheeks, and flicked her gaze up to his where what she saw sent goosebumps scattering across her skin beneath the draping silk from her shoulders to her sleeves.

She watched as his gaze searched her from head to toe. Was he disappointed that she hadn't picked one of the dresses he had pulled for her? Was he angry that she'd found the one that he'd discarded?

Why was it that she could never tell with him? she cursed mentally. Why was he just so hard for her to read? He'd been so kind to her last night. After she'd finished crying, he'd walked her to the room he'd arranged for her and left her at the doorway. It had been naive, and supremely silly to hope that he might have stayed. Might have…

And he'd been gone before she could even ask about the wedding night. She'd been so intensely focused on putting one foot in front of the other, that if she wasn't careful, she'd end up like her mother. No. After today, after the marriage, she would find a way to claw back her independence. She had to. For herself and more importantly for her child.

She reached the top of the aisle and felt Micha's assessing gaze on her, as if he'd noticed a change in her demeanour. As the priest welcomed them, and the congregation, she held her soon-to-be husband's gaze. Looking, really looking this time. Not shying away or getting distracted by other things.

There were things she knew, the golden flecks in eyes so dark they almost looked black. The small flat mole just beneath his left eye, and the tiny silvery scar through his eyebrow on the right, where the hair didn't quite grow back as thickly. All these things were familiar, but she wanted more.

He held her gaze through her silent investigation, a raised eyebrow, rueful, challenging and open. As if he was saying, *Have at it, look* all *you want*. It was a dare, like when they'd been kids, and a strange wave of humour swept over them, pulled at the edges of his mouth, just as it drew on her heart. Her mouth wobbled, trying not to smile. And then it passed, just like the tide, leaving a long stretch of emptiness behind it. The smile fell from her lips and the humour from her heart.

She watched the little curve at the edge of his lip flatten, as a sense of weight, of heaviness settled between them. Seriousness. Something old and something responsible. As if she felt all the years since their childhood pass between them in just a few seconds.

And then she was hit by such an intense wave of longing. Oh, nothing like Paris, nothing as obvious as attraction. But for what they could have had. What it could have been. It could have been something beautiful between them. If he hadn't left her. If he hadn't chosen Gio over her, just like every other member of her family. They could have had *this*. And it could have been so wonderful. This time, the wave brought sadness and loss. An older grief, just as known, just as familiar, a sadness she'd never quite got over.

As the faint smell of incense and candle wax mixed with the wildflowers from her bouquet, and the priest pressed on with readings as familiar to her as the names of her family members, she saw it in his gaze too. The hurt, the anger, the sadness. The *loss*.

His naked emotions shocked her, but not enough to override the rising anger. He looked at her as if it were *her* fault. As if *she'd* done this to them. But she hadn't. *He* was the one who had left. *He* was the one who had disappeared off the face of the planet, so that she'd been alone with no one to count on but herself.

'Do you have the rings?'

The priest's question jerked her out of her thoughts, severing the strange, hypnotic moment that had locked them together, excluding everyone around them.

She turned to look at where Ivy and Antonio sat in the front pew—her stony-faced parents on the other side of the aisle. Everyone was either grim faced or fascinated, as if waiting to see if she would really go through with it.

Her gaze returned to Micha, who reached into his pocket and retrieved a small black velvet box without missing a beat. As if they hadn't just shared…*something*.

She just about stopped herself from pressing her hand to her stomach, to their child, to reassure them both that this was the right thing to do, that this would give them the protection and security they would desperately need if the Gallos decided to turn against them.

The priest continued with the ceremony, sharing words

of commitment, of love, of honour, and she wondered whether she would ever have those things now. He despised her. That's what she'd seen in the emotions Micha kept locked away. He resented her for this. But it didn't matter, because she knew that he would love their child with the same fierceness and that was all she needed, she told herself as she repeated after the priest, 'I do.'

Micha had kept quiet, even for him, throughout the short reception that had followed. Well. The reception was short for him and Maria. By all accounts the Gallos were drinking the bar dry at his considerable expense.

'Do you not think they'll notice if we leave so early?'

It was the last thing she'd said to him, which was perhaps not that surprising given his response.

'Do you think a single one of them will actually care?'

The moment the car had pulled into the gated driveway of his villa, he'd flung the door to the car open and stepped out into the night. *Cristo*, he needed a drink. He'd not trusted himself or them to have one in front of the Gallos at the reception, and now...? Well, Maria was now a Rufina, he supposed. If she chose to take his name.

The thought pulled him up short, but he dismissed it as a problem for another day. Without waiting to see if she followed him, Micha marched up the stone steps to where the large front door was being held open by his housekeeper.

'*Felicitazioni!*' Benito proclaimed, ignoring both Micha's frown and the growl that would have scared a lesser man. But Benito had been with him for nearly eight years now, and had seen pretty much all there was to see.

What little was left of Micha's conscience forced his

steps to slow and to at least ensure that Benito greeted his new wife—his *wife*—with the respect that her family clearly hadn't afforded her.

'Signora, welcome home,' Benito said.

The words struck Micha like an anvil, and for a single moment, his eyes connected with hers, took in the sight of her in a wedding dress, hovering on the threshold to his home, *her home*, before he let out another growl, stalked into his study and slammed the door behind him.

Of course, he should have known better than to think that Maria would leave him to his peace.

Less than five seconds later, she threw the door back open, only to come into the office and slam it behind her. It had taken more than he'd care to admit to stop himself from flinching from the sound of the door hurtling against its frame.

She stood there like one of the furies, her fists on her hips, glaring at him as if she had the right to be mad at *him*.

'Go to bed, Maria. It's too late for this.'

She opened her mouth and then closed it again. Before opening it and then closing it one more time.

'How…how dare you send me to bed like a *child*,' she whisper-hissed.

How dare he? *Cristo*, if she only knew that he was trying to spare her from the thoughts he was struggling to contain.

'*Va bene*. Out with it,' he commanded.

'You can't ignore me like this, Micha. You've been furious with me all afternoon. You didn't say a single thing to me through the wedding breakfast or reception.'

He shrugged off his tux jacket. 'And?' he said with his back to her.

'And?' she asked, eyebrow arched in surprise. 'So much for *everyone believing this marriage is real*,' she said.

He clenched his teeth together and turned, leaning back against the table.

'Don't do that.' She gestured angrily to where he perched and turned her back on him.

'Do what?' he demanded.

'Do *that*, lean back like *that*.'

'*Madonna mia*, Maria, this is my office, and I just need—'

'What? *What* is it that you need? *Tonight*. On your *wedding night*?' she demanded angrily.

'Space!' he shouted, swallowing immediately and regretting his outburst. It wasn't that he was angry. It was that it was uncontrolled, and she would know that and he was so tired of fighting her.

'Do you think I wanted this?' she accused.

'Do you think *I* did?' he fired back. 'Seriously Maria, do you think that I wanted this either? Me, whose mother had to sell her own body to put food in my mouth. Do you think that I would have ever, *ever*, wanted to force a woman to marry me?'

The shock on Maria's face would have stopped his words, if it hadn't been for the fact that the dam was well and truly burst and now everything was pouring out.

'Just the thought of it *horrifies* me, Maria. It fills me with the kind of self-hatred I wouldn't wish on anyone,' he growled, slashing his hand through the air between them.

'I *will* do everything in my power to protect you and our child, but damn it Maria, do you actually think I'm *enjoying* this? Contrary to what you and your family think, I'm not actually a monster and I do *not* enjoy forcing women against their will to do something they don't want to do. Of course, I appreciate that it would be hard, no, near on *impossible*, for you to credit that one day, *one day*, I might actually have wanted to be with someone who had chosen to be with me because they cared for me. And now, that is impossible.'

He shook his head and huffed out a bitter laugh.

'I could never bring myself to regret what happened in Paris,' he admitted, 'because I would *never* regret what led to the birth of our child. But by my word, I wish you'd never come to my office that night.'

For just a moment, he thought he might have seen a flash of hurt in her gaze, but he must have been imagining it. He stared into the fire that Benito had lit just before they'd arrived.

Maria stared at him, her aching heart bound by the confining silk of the wedding dress as she drew in breath after breath as if she'd run a marathon. She knew, in that moment, that she would never forget his words as long as she lived.

He was, just like her, trapped. Not by their child, but by this situation that had spun so wildly out of control. She wanted to cry just from the agony in his tone when the confession that he'd hated himself that much was wrenched from his soul. She could see it. Could see the torture pulling him from each side. The need to be a better parent, a better *man* than the bastard that had abandoned him and his mother, but the anathema of having forced her to marry him had damned him all the same.

And she was more than just complicit in that. She was integral. She had done that to him.

Guilt came thick and fast. *She* had done it to them when she'd gone to Paris determined to punish him. All she'd wanted was some kind of reckoning for her broken teenage heart, and instead, she'd doomed them both. But despite the shocking vehemence of his words, she couldn't leave it like this. She couldn't let him ignore her like her father, and she couldn't say nothing like her mother.

'But I did,' she said, finally coming back to his wish that she'd never come to his office that night in Paris. 'And I am carrying our child. And now, we're married. And I...' She hesitated, but pushed on. Because she needed to. Because their child needed her to. 'And I don't know where I'm supposed to go. I don't know where I'm sleeping. I don't know if you want—' Maria swallowed '—*expected* to share a bed. I don't know if we're going on a honeymoon. I don't know what I'm going to do when we come back from a honeymoon if we do go on one. I don't know *anything*, Micha, because you are not talking to me. And you need to talk to me. I can't...' The words caught in her throat.

He looked up at her then, his expression unreadable. He had given her his truth. It was the least she could do for him.

'I can't have a marriage like my parents,' she said, swallowing her shame and her hurt.

After a beat, he nodded slowly. He knew what she meant. Knew how much her parents' marriage had haunted her. Her stay-at-home mother, who had nothing and no one to distract her from her husband's abandonment. Her uncaring and unfeeling father. *Cristo*, she'd told him enough of her childhood hurts back when they'd been teenagers and in love. Or thought they were in love. Could it really have been that easy back then? Could they have made a real go of it? If he hadn't left? If Gio hadn't sent him away?

If she'd gone after him?

'You were the one who wanted everyone to believe that this is a love match. I can work with that. But you need to help me. I can't keep running along behind you playing catch-up to whatever you deem I need to know when you think I need to know it. The wedding was one thing,' she conceded. But now that she was here, now that her mind had caught up, she couldn't sit back and let things happen to her. She hadn't before Paris and she shouldn't now. 'But the future is another. And I want to be partners,' she said defiantly.

She let him gaze at her. There was nothing left to hide, nothing to conceal. She'd meant every word she'd said.

Again, he nodded slowly. With the firelight on the planes of his face, handsome didn't even begin to describe the complexities of what he looked like to her. Familiar. Infuriating. Arousing. Angering. Powerful. Resentful.

'London.'

'London?' she repeated, bringing her out of the spell cast by the shadows of the fire.

'Our honeymoon. We're going to London. It would have been Hawaii, but your father had other ideas.'

'My father?' Maria asked, feeling her face scrunch in confusion.

'It seems that he is trying to get to me through Peterson, which perhaps wouldn't have been possible if I'd been able to secure the contract with your help before now.'

She dismissed the light jab that she was—in some small way—to blame. In part because she knew it was true.

'Why would he do that?' she asked.

'I'm not quite sure,' he said, finally standing up away from the desk. 'But first we need to pay Peterson a visit and get him back in line. Or the Gallos will have much, much more to talk about than our wedding. They'll be sitting back and watching the end of Gallo Group altogether.'

'Okay,' she answered decisively. Gallo Group was where she felt strong. Where she knew what she was doing. 'Do you want me to arrange a meeting with him or do you think it would be better coming from you?' Maria asked.

'I think it would be even better coming from GG's chief financial officer.'

'Of course,' Maria said, nodding in agreement and looking away so he couldn't see the slight wince of hurt she felt at her offer being rejected. 'Is that Giovanni?'

'No.'

'Then who?'

'You.'

Maria frowned. 'What?'

'If you'll have it, of course. Giovanni will be on hand through whatever maternity leave you'd like to have, but he's more than happy to step aside.'

'I thought he wanted the job.'

'He did. Until he realised just how awful the Gallos can be,' Micha said, rubbing a hand over the back of his head.

'When did you decide this?' Maria asked through the thickening of her throat. She'd hate it if it had been last night, because of her father. She hated that he was the one to give her the position in the first place, but she'd meant what she said. She and Micha needed to start working together, so it really didn't matter what his answer was.

'Before I found you in Trasimeno.'

The day she'd tried to kick him out before hearing what he had to say because she was so worried about him finding out about the baby.

She pressed a hand to her mouth. Oh god, how had they made a mess of so much?

He came to stand in front of her, something like acceptance in his eyes.

'Together.'

It was the echo of a promise they'd once made too many years ago now to count. It was both hurt and heartfelt, and she welcomed it as much as she could.

'Together.'

CHAPTER NINE

'AND THAT'S WHEN I told him he had a deal!' exclaimed Daniel Peterson.

He might not look it, dressed in an off-the-rack grey suit, a white-and-grey-striped shirt and a pink tie that aged him horribly, but Daniel Peterson was one of the richest men in Europe. It was, Maria realised, his own type of armour. He delighted in being underestimated and unfortunately Micha had committed less of a sin, and more the fulfilment of Daniel's often persecutory expectations, ones that told him he would constantly be undervalued and insignificant to younger and brighter men than him. Peterson's ego was often his downfall, but surprisingly enough, his intelligence was high enough to drag him back up again. It was just that most people didn't stick around long enough to find out that this was the case, until they had been dismissed by Daniel.

'Not bad, Daniel,' Maria offered, her smile wry, just the way the Englishman liked it. It hid the tiredness that was beginning to press against the backs of her eyes and she was fighting the urge to place a hand around her stomach. There was nothing there other than a bundle of cells, but she had walked into the restaurant at the top of the Shard feeling protective of those cells. As if she was being reminded that having both a career and motherhood was going to be difficult.

Micha had been content to let her take the lead. Something that surprised her. Oh yes, he'd said as much, but in Maria's experience, the men of Gallo Group often said one thing and did another. And this was, actually, the first time they'd worked together in the years since they'd both worked for her grandfather.

Unbidden, her gaze flicked between the two men. There was no contest. It had nothing to do with the fact that Peterson was nearly nine years her senior, or greying at the temples. Some would find that eminently attractive. But Micha?

She took a sip of her sparkling water.

It did nothing to wash away the taste of desire on her tongue. His jaw in dark shadow seemed arrogant rather than lazy, the high cheekbones sculpting the planes of his face in harsh lines, the furrowed brow only serving to draw attention rather than deter it.

Husband. Lover. Father of her child. Enemy.

Micha had been many things over the years, but she was finding it hard to pin down just what he was to her *now*.

She sighed.

'Ahh, is it that time already?' Daniel asked, misunderstanding her feelings. But she could work with this so she smiled and agreed that 'yes. The wining and dining is done, and now we talk business.'

'Okay,' he said, smoothing his fingers along the edge of the white-cloth-covered table.

The darkness of the night beyond the extremely thick windows, the subtle lighting and gentle hum of conversation, as well as the discreet positioning of the table, added to a feeling of seclusion; as if it were just the three of them.

'I heard there was a mistake during the contract negotiations,' Maria started, ignoring the slightest flinch from Micha, without taking her eyes off Daniel. 'And I'd like to hear how you felt it came about.'

'We agreed verbally, to continue in the manner as before. And yet when we received the contract, key components had been changed.'

'What were you told?'

Daniel flicked his gaze to Micha before it returned to Maria.

'That it was a mistake with a new member of staff.'

'You didn't believe this?'

'What I didn't believe was that such an important contract for Gallo Group had been put under the charge of a member of staff so inexperienced as to make such mistakes. It shows a distinct lack of respect.'

'Mmm.'

Maria took another sip of her water, buying herself some time. She knew what had happened—Micha had told her as much—she just wanted to see how Daniel saw it. Needed to, in order to know whether the plan she had to rectify it would work.

'Mmm?' Daniel questioned.

'Yes. Mmm. I am thinking. I am also wondering if you know how many contracts GG was dealing with at that specific time, given the transition of power from my grandfather to the man he chose to follow in his footsteps.'

'If that had been the case, I might have been more understanding, but I'd heard rumours.'

Maria cut a glance to Micha, who, this time, was not just frowning, but positively scowling.

'Rumours that suggested that you, and not Mr Rufina, were Gio's intended heir.'

Maria silently cursed. It wasn't Micha who would be the downfall of this company, but whatever member of her family had a big mouth and seemed intent on letting the whole thing burn rather than trying to save it.

'But you are back. Wife and CFO. That could change things.'

She hoped to god that the dim lighting in the restaurant hid the blush of anger painting her cheeks. Of course, a man would see her marriage first. She opened her mouth to speak but Micha got there first.

'I think you'll find, Mr Peterson, that marriage to me comes a lot further down the list of Maria's priorities than Gallo Group.' Micha's voice was low, but cutting. But not to her. The cut was to him. To Peterson. The man who they had come here intending to woo. 'And if you don't see that, and don't want to continue with Gallo Group with Maria as CFO, secure in the knowledge that under her, your wealth will increase exponentially, then I'm not entirely sure that we want to do business with you,' he said, leaning back in his chair. 'Now, I understand your concern. Reading over a contract that differed to our verbal agreement must have been jarring. However, like Gio, I strongly believe in giving chances to staff, letting them try and letting them learn. And lessons were learned. The staff member is still in our employ and has not—in fact—made another mistake yet, despite working on multiple contracts simultaneously. You can be assured, he never will.

'Now the question moves to whether *I* want to work with someone who gets their—how do the English say?—knickers in a twist because a new hire used the wrong contract template. This speaks to me of someone *ungracious*.'

'Micha,' Maria cut in from across the table in warning. He had made his point. Rubbing Daniel's nose in it wouldn't help at all.

'Darling,' he bit back with a sinful smile.

She turned to Peterson. 'He is being defensive on my behalf.'

Daniel grinned. 'As he should, and very much as I'd hoped he would be. Maria, I hope you know me well enough to know that I am completely aware of your skills and your contribution to Gallo Group and would never dismiss you as "just a wife." I just wanted to see how that dynamic would play out. So, okay, you have me intrigued. I want to know what your new offer is.'

'Why should we make any changes to the original terms?' Maria asked, her words clear as a bell.

'Because I know how much you need me,' Daniel said.

'*Needed*. We have, of course, in the last few months been exploring other avenues,' Maria lied without compunction.

Daniel raised an eyebrow, willing to entertain the threat that Maria had dangled before him, like the stick instead of the carrot, and Micha didn't know whether to be impressed, or infuriated, but he was willing to see how this played out.

'I don't believe you,' the Englishman said slowly.

'That's irrelevant. We have been exploring a rebranding. Clearly there are people who have had some difficulties reacting to the changing of the guard, which leaves us with two options. To hold fast, *or...*'

'We completely rebrand. Fresh blood, new contracts, new appearance,' Micha picked up seamlessly.

'You wouldn't. That's crazy,' Daniel said with a shake of his head.

'No, it's a gamble. And one that could very well pay off. There are quite a number of people out there who are getting tired of fusty old men making the same decisions over and over and over again,' Maria interjected.

'And some people are attracted to a little bit of crazy,' Micha replied with an arrogant smirk, sure to exacerbate the rumours of his rebellious business sense.

'And the board?' Daniel asked pointedly.

'Will fall in line,' Maria replied with all the confidence that Micha didn't believe for a single second.

Peterson leaned back in his chair, his gaze flicking between Maria and Micha. A waiter approached, and veered swiftly away with a single flick of Peterson's hand.

'Mmm.' The sound was almost a growl. And almost approving. 'You work horribly well together. And I'd rather be on your side than against it.' With a nod, he stood from the table. 'I believe I have taken up enough of your honeymoon as it is.' Peterson cast a look between them. 'I will happily sign on the terms as originally agreed. But I leave you with a warning. Someone is stirring the pot. And you need to find out who, or there won't be a company for me to sign with.'

He left Maria and Micha in stunned silence with empty dessert plates in front of them, which the waiter came to take away as Maria struggled to catch up with what had just happened.

'He's right,' Micha said, his gaze heavy on her.

'About a traitor?'

Micha held her gaze. 'No. That we work well together.'

He meant it. He'd enjoyed working with her. They'd never done it before, their past a wedge between them like an iceberg, forcing them to only interact when necessary. Gio had been content to leave Paris and England under his purview, and Micha had left the financial discussions between his manager and Maria to get on with.

Oh, he'd known she was good, but seeing it in action, it was a rush. Firing his blood stream. Ignoring it, he signalled for the cheque, and led her out of the impressive London Shard, which reached into the night sky above them as their car drew up to the pavement to pick them up. His hand hovered at the base of her spine as he guided her into the back of the car, his palm tingling. He flexed it open and closed before he slipped in beside her.

As the car wound its way through dark London streets he wondered whether they maintained their silence because of the driver, or because it was easier that way. They really only seemed to encounter difficulties when they spoke to each other.

There hadn't been a huge amount of speaking in Paris though. The swift lightning strike of arousal forked down into a simmering sea and he turned to look out of the window and away from her.

It didn't take long for the car to reach the apartment he kept in Notting Hill. While he'd been in Paris, it had made sense, especially with the amount of business that Gallo Group had with British clients. He hadn't been here for nearly eight months. The last time had been...the last time he'd seen Gio, he realised with a thud of his heart.

His feelings about the old man had always been complex. But above all, Gio had taught Micha nearly everything he knew. And Gio had appreciated what he hadn't taught him; what had been pure instinct for Micha. *You're like me, you know? And I like that.* But it hadn't been enough to make him worthy of the man's granddaughter.

As the car drew to a stop, Micha exited and held the door open for Maria, his hand waiting for hers. After a moment where he thought she might refuse, she accepted it and let him lead her up to the slick black-painted door, where he entered the pin on the keypad and ushered her over the threshold.

Maria blinked in the harsh lighting as they took the red-carpeted stairs all the way up to the third floor. A part of him wanted to see her expression as she took in his apartment. Of all of the places he'd lived, this was his. Not Gio's, not the Gallos'. He hadn't even tried to make his home in Italy—a place that had always marginalised him for his mixed European heritage. But here, in London, the melting pot of cultures and nationalities, he'd made it his home. At extreme expense of course.

It was an 'upside down' apartment, in that the door opened onto a hallway where a set of stairs would take you to the sitting room and open-plan kitchen on the floor above, while straight ahead the door was open onto a large bedroom suite and off to the left was a bathroom.

Without waiting for him, she took the stairs and came to a stop, forcing him to pause behind her where he could see the open-plan living area that had stunned her. He knew the feeling. It was precisely why he'd fallen in love with the building.

Glass fronted three whole sides of the room, London lit up against the night sky surrounding them almost entirely. A large U-shaped sofa faced, not the room, but the view beyond, making one feel as if they were at the very tip of the skyline looking out across the city in all its splendour.

'Would you like something to drink?' he asked.

'Herbal tea if you have it,' she said, unable to tear her gaze away from the sight. Two sides of the view had strips of decking, where there were large green plants in giant tubs, and chairs, and a table where he often liked to have his morning coffee, no matter the weather.

She went to the window, with her arms wrapped around herself as he made a cup of chamomile and himself a decaf espresso.

'You shouldn't have done that, you know.'

Her words carried easily across the room. It was a reprimand, but it had no sting to it. No heat.

'It was reckless to call Daniel out like that. His ego is as precious to him as his billions. It could have backfired terribly.'

'But it didn't. You saw to that,' he said, picking up their drinks and moving to the large sofa that was perhaps his most favourite possession oddly.

He placed the hot drinks down on the coffee table and sat.

She looked tired, he realised, and wondered how much she was hiding from him, whether the pregnancy was hitting her harder than she was letting on.

'My mother,' he started, swallowing his natural inclination *not* to talk, not to open himself up and be vulnerable with Maria, because of how much it had cost him when she'd cut him from her life before. 'She had terribly swollen ankles with me. And awful morning sickness.'

Maria heard the lifeline he was extending to her. She felt the hesitancy in him, but appreciated his effort. It wasn't as if either of them found it easy. Not after the decades of hurt and resentment that piled in between them.

'I'm actually not feeling too bad,' she offered him, turning back to the room and leaving the nightscape of London behind her. 'Tired, yes, but okay.'

She sat on one corner of the U-shaped sofa, absently rubbing her hand over the warm smooth leather beneath her palm. She didn't know why she found it soothing, but she'd been doing it ever since she found out she was pregnant.

'Do you have any appointments lined up? Scans or such?'

'They're scheduled for when I'm back.'

'Could I...?' He stopped, cleared his throat.

Instead of rushing him or filling in for him, she waited, remembering this from years ago. Remembering how much he hated people doing that for him. And remembering how Gio was the only one who let him take his time apart from her. Did he miss him? Did Micha miss Gio the way that she missed Gio? Messily? With difficulty? Because he'd been a hard man to love, but also almost impossible not to.

'Could I come with you?'

'Yes. I would like that,' she said, hating that he'd had to ask, knowing how much that would have cost him. That that was how bad things were between them. They were married. They were going to be parents, for heaven's sake. They had to do better than this.

'If there's anything you need, Maria, just ask. Please.'

'I…'

'Yes?'

'I would like us to have a honeymoon.'

'We are—'

'Not one that involves work.'

He raised an eyebrow at her, accusingly. Yes, she found it *just as* ironic as he did that *she* was the one requesting that they take time off work. But maybe just maybe, away from everything they could find some equilibrium. She swept a hand unconsciously over her abdomen, the strange firmness there new and unusual, but full of just so much that she was almost terrified of messing things up. And she really didn't want that.

'Okay, a honeymoon,' he agreed, nodding.

'And… I want us to find a new home.'

This time his brows shot up into his hair line.

'Really?'

'Obviously I'm not expecting you to pay for it—'

'I can pay for it Maria,' he growled, interrupting her. 'What's wrong with my villa?'

'It's *yours*. Not *ours*. I feel like…' She'd felt like a fool, the night of her wedding. But she couldn't admit that to him. A silly bride, having expected more than a bed in a spare room. She swallowed. 'I feel like a guest.'

He frowned. 'I didn't mean for that.'

'I know,' she replied honestly. 'But… I think we need a fresh start. A new beginning. As equals as much as partners, and as confidants as much as—' She'd been about to say *lovers*. But they weren't lovers. He couldn't even bring himself to touch her. And she hated that she knew that. Tiny little tremors fissured out from the cracks in her heart. He hadn't touched her since the priest had them kiss to secure their vows. And that had been as cold as a fish.

'I will get my assistant to start looking once you give him a list of your requirements.'

'Our.'

He blinked at her.

'Our requirements. And I don't want your assistant to do it, I want to do it *together*.'

He bit his lip and nodded. '*Va bene*. Is there anything else?'

There was, but she was not at all sure either of them was ready for her request. Yet, if she didn't speak now, when would she? Would she become like her mother, sitting in silence waiting for her husband to suddenly start caring about her?

'You agreed that I wouldn't have a marriage like my parents.'

His eyes narrowed. He seemed almost preternaturally still.

'Yet that is what you gave me the night of our wedding,' she said, her insides trembling, worried about what she was asking for. Because that night was something she had absolutely no intention of repeating. Removing the gown herself, in an empty bedroom, all by herself, had been...devastating. She'd scrubbed at the tears that she'd kept silent, and burrowed into the bed beneath the duvet, red eyed and hollow hearted, all the way to dawn.

Micha might have demanded that they work together, but he had remained utterly removed from her in every other way. But she couldn't live like this. Couldn't bear to.

She'd grown up in the shadow of her mother's silence, and her father's absence. It was the one thing, the *one* thing, she'd never wanted for herself. Oh, theirs wouldn't be a normal marriage. How could it be? But that didn't mean they couldn't have companionship, or…or… Her heart stumbled over itself.

'I… I don't know what you mean, what you're asking me for,' he said, slowly as if just as fearful of where this would go.

'I want more. More than just a marriage that looks good on the outside.'

'More,' he repeated dully.

Oh, for god's sake, she internally cried. *Why are you making me say it?*

'You want to share a bed?' he asked, his voice gravel and sending invisible shivers across her skin, which was nonsense, because she was pretty sure that he'd not lay a single finger on her in that way ever again.

'Yes.'

'Yes?'

'Yes,' she confirmed, with a raised eyebrow, daring him to ask for even more damn clarifications.

He opened his mouth and closed it again, and honestly if it wasn't for how insecure it made her feel, the entire thing would almost be funny. She'd not exactly ever thought herself to be in the position of negotiating billion-dollar deals one minute and then half of a marital bed the next. But here she was, doing precisely that.

'You said we'd work together. I want that. We're married. We're a team. And we're going to be parents, to our child, who will need us to be together.'

'Starting…?'

'Is there a reason it shouldn't be tonight?' she asked with a lot more bravado than she felt. She was beginning to regret her decision to confront him about it. Until she remembered the hollow ache in her chest only the night before.

'No?'

'Is that a question or an answer Micha, because honestly—'

'No, it's an answer.'

'As in no you won't let me share your bed? Micha, I swear you make things so unnecessarily—'

'Are you finished?' he asked, coming to his full height, holding his hand out for her to take.

Now she was the one with her mouth hanging open like a fish, which she promptly shut with a snap. She looked up at him, knowing that this was new for them. New territory, new dynamics.

This is what you wanted, right?

Wanted? No. Needed? Yes.

And she did need it. They both did.

She placed her hand in his, heart beating, and let him gently pull her up from the seat. They were closer than they'd been even at the church as they shared their vows. From here, she could see the little jagged line of silver through his right eyebrow and stupidly wanted to trace it with her thumb.

But couldn't. Couldn't because she had to claw to claim only just a little. Because she got the sense that if she moved too quickly, or too far, he'd disappear from her like a mirage. The golden flecks in his eyes spun out like a snowstorm, making her wonder at all the words he was thinking that couldn't get past his ironclad control.

'Are you ready?' he asked, swiftly adding 'to sleep,' as if she needed the clarification.

She nodded, truthfully, as a wave of near exhaustion threatened to overwhelm her, and let him lead her back down the stairs to the bedroom.

She held herself back on the threshold, knowing she had no right to ask, but unable to move forward until she had.

'Have you...have you, with other women?' Oh god, why was she making such a hash of this?

'No. No one else has been in this bed, save me.'

Micha didn't know whether he'd needed to say it as much as she'd needed to hear it, but he felt some of the tension ease following his statement.

He'd expected her to scoff, or question him, but he realised that that expectation wasn't actually based on *this* Maria. But the Maria from before. The middle Maria, he was beginning to think of as the person he'd avoided for eleven years. The one that had, whenever they'd come into contact, bit and hissed like a cat. *This* Maria was different and different again to the young Maria he'd once known, and maybe he owed it to both them and their unborn child to get to know her.

'You can use the bathroom first if you'd like?' he offered, and she nodded and took her toiletries into the bathroom that was accessed from back out in the hall.

He stared at the bed almost resentfully. He'd planned to sleep on the sofa, obviously not enough of a bastard to make his pregnant wife unhappy. But she'd been unhappy the night of her wedding. His conscience twisted. Angry, furious, frustrated, all things he was very familiar with feeling over the last eleven years. But he'd not once felt *bad*.

Until now.

She'd had to ask for a damn honeymoon.

She'd felt like a stranger in his home, which—of course—she *would* have.

He was on the brink of really messing things up. He could feel it.

He imagined her washing her face, brushing her teeth, these deeply intimate moments of married life that others took for granted, and he just didn't know whether he was hiding in this room because he didn't want that, or because he wanted it so badly.

The door behind him pushed open, and her face glistened like dew, all make-up removed. She was wearing a little vest thing and a pair of silk black pants and she'd never looked more beautiful.

'I'll just...' he trailed off and backed out to the bathroom, the minty scent of her toothpaste in the air, the sink wet from where she'd run the taps.

He gripped the vanity, knuckles white, head bowed.

Get it together. Get it goddamn together.

Sharing a bed with Maria would be the sweetest of tortures. To be that close to her, her warmth, the smoothness of her skin. Not once had he forgotten the feel of her beneath his hands, on his tongue, around him.

She'd asked him for a real relationship, but in order for him to give that to her, he was going to have to let her in. But he wasn't sure he could do that. He'd barely survived the last time they'd broken up. Gio and the work he'd made Micha do was the only thing that had pulled him through the days, weeks and months that followed his move to Paris.

Only, this time there wasn't even a choice. They were going to have a child.

I'll do whatever it takes.

His own words, delivered as a threat, come back to haunt him.

A short while later he returned to the bedroom to find Maria already under the covers, the night lamp on that side of the room already switched off.

He sat heavily on the opposite side of the bed.

'Is this okay?' she asked quietly. 'I don't know what side—'

'It's fine,' he hastily assured her, wincing when he realised he'd cut her off.

'Oh. Okay. Good night then.'

'Good night, Maria,' he said, as he slipped beneath the covers, the distance between them an insurmountable divide. The fear that, in the night, he might accidentally reach for her terrified him. His muscles locked, not even wanting to breathe loudly in case it disturbed her.

Long into the night and the early morning, he remained awake, planning the honeymoon she'd asked for as something to do. He would absolutely do what she wanted, the honeymoon, the new home, the fresh start…but he knew with a high degree of certainty that he'd lose his heart in the process.

Just like he had before.

CHAPTER TEN

MICHA HAD WATCHED Maria try to get comfortable in the private jet's seat for the last ten minutes.

'Do you want to swap?' he asked, finally.

'No, I don't think that would make much of a difference,' she admitted, still clearly uncomfortable.

He was guessing that it was her back, because she hadn't let him know what it was that she was finding uncomfortable and he fought the ridiculous—and frankly dangerous—desire to tell her to *use her words*.

She shot him a look from under her eyelashes. 'Are you going to tell me *now*, where we're going?' she asked.

He pursed his lips and shook his head. She sighed dramatically and he bit back a smile.

Their morning had proceeded as much as their night had. Going through the motions of getting ready for the day, while painfully conscious of each other, both aware it was strange and awkward and neither really knowing what to do about it except press on until it wasn't.

'Not even a hint?' Maria asked from across the cabin.

He opened his mouth to say it was somewhere she had always wanted to go, and then realised that she may have already been there. With someone else. His mouth shut with a snap. She frowned at him and then eventually looked out the window.

He'd been oddly pleased with his two-o'clock-in-the-morning idea of coming here. He'd dimmed the brightness of his phone screen so as not to wake her as he made the *incredibly* last minute booking, and notified the staff of the jet. All of whom would be handsomely recompensed for the change in itinerary.

But just the thought, the mere possibility, that she'd already come here with someone else was enough to sour his mood significantly. Which was nothing but a slightly bruised ego, he told himself sternly. He just had to get over it. And if she asked him about it? Reminded him that she'd once told him how much she wanted to come here? He'd lie and tell her it was just a happy accident.

They landed three hours later, Maria peering out of the small cabin windows to try and identify where they were from what little she could see.

'Oh!' she exclaimed as they were hit with a wall of heat the moment the flight attendant opened the door for them. Maria looked back at him, something like excitement and hope shining in her gaze.

'You didn't,' she accused.

'Well, as I'm not one hundred percent sure what you think I might have not done, I—'

'Oh,' she said again, with such sheer delight it left him speechless. He hadn't heard her sound like that since they were both teenagers.

If the palm trees planted around the lowslung building that formed Manera Airport hadn't given it away then Welcome to Al-Maghrib did it. The architectural design criss-crossing the front and sides of the building was impressive and eye-catching.

Maria was almost jumping up and down on the spot with excitement, in direct contrast to how she'd been on the plane and for the first time since last night, maybe longer, a thin thread of tension unspooled from deep within him. He'd done the right thing. Even if she had come here with someone else. As staff checked their passports and luggage, she raised onto her tiptoes and whispered in his ear.

'You remembered.'

'I don't know what you're talking about,' he denied.

'I don't believe you,' she said with the biggest smile. 'Thank you.'

He allowed a smile to pull at one corner of his mouth and she raised an eyebrow and pointed at him. 'I don't believe you,' she mouthed as she accepted her passport back from the administrator and went to peer through the window that looked out at the city of Marrakesh.

It wasn't long before they were on their way in a chauffeur driven car towards their destination. A lot of the main hotels on the strip were luxurious to the extreme, but Micha had wanted something more... His mind skated over the word *intimate* and chose *private* instead.

And the private villa, half an hour away from the city, on the grounds of what had once been a palace, had caught his eye immediately. It was modest in size, but absolutely outstanding in terms of amenities. Not only was there a bedroom suite, there was also a separate suite for massage and pampering treatments, a private pool, a personal chef, and twenty-four-hour waitstaff. No expense had been spared. Less than five hours after leaving London, Micha and Maria stepped out of the car and into paradise.

They both just stood there for a moment. The carved detail around the flat roof of the one-storey building filtered the setting sun's rays like a cut-out paper lantern, glowing a beautiful orange yellow, before the gaze was drawn to the sea.

Micha felt the breath sigh out of him, as if the tension was beginning to leave his body just at the sight of it. He'd never come here. Never been able to, after how they'd left things. But now he was here with Maria it felt...*right*.

Maria couldn't help herself. From the moment they were welcomed into the villa, she just felt thrilled. The interior design was incredible, brass finishings, incredible detailed cut-outs in the panels that divided living areas, or shielded lamps, or the exquisite tiles in a bathroom that was near pornographic in its luxury. The bath was sunken into the floor, and little sconces held flickering flames already lit, the scent of rose in the air, and petals dancing on the water.

But beyond all of that was the fact that he'd remembered. And instead of trying to hide how that made her feel, she welcomed it, let it warm her like the ambient temperature around her, so much more pleasant than London had been.

'Dinner will be served in a short while out on the terrace,' the house staff member announced before disappearing magically.

'Where does he go?' Maria whispered to Micha when they were left on their own.

'There are hidden rooms in the walls,' he replied with

such a dead tone that her gaze snapped up to his in shock, only to find laughter dancing in his eyes.

She smiled, tried to hide it behind her hand and then wondered why she should be so embarrassed.

He caught her hand just as she was about to pull it away.

'You don't have to do that. You don't have to hide your smile from me,' he said, his burnished gaze becoming serious.

She nodded, her heart leaping. She remembered. Remembered how he would look at her when she laughed. As if she were the most incredible thing he'd ever seen. He'd do and say silly things just to make her laugh. As if her pleasure was his.

She swallowed, her heart turning in her chest. 'I'm going to get changed for dinner,' she said, slipping from the room before he could divine her thoughts.

When she had packed for the trip to London, she had thought it would just be a few nights there and that they'd return. She'd have to buy some clothes to get her through the stay here.

Twelve nights, he'd told her. Twelve nights in a North African palace. That's what it felt like. The grandeur was more than she'd ever seen as a Gallo. She sighed a little sadly at her clothing. It was unsuitable, either for Marrakesh or her feelings about what she wanted to look like. She sighed and opened the wardrobe to hang up her shirt before it crumpled and gasped.

Her phone buzzed.

I hope you don't mind. I took the liberty of arranging

some appropriate clothes for us. We can shop for more if none of these suit, I just wanted you to be comfortable.

From Micha, it was a veritable essay. But before she could ponder on how much easier it would be to talk to him over text message, her gaze was drawn to the beautiful clothes he'd arranged for her.

She loved them *all*. Colourful silks, all suiting her skin tone, hung in draped layers, soft easy clothes for lounging, all impeccable quality and incredible design—sleek, sophisticated, but just a little softer than perhaps she would have chosen for herself, and somehow more fitting. She wanted that softness.

When had she grown tired of the severe armour she'd felt necessary to wear around the men in Gallo Group? How long had she stifled that softness in order not to appear weak? And how ironic, that this was what was going to set off an existential crisis for her—and not her pregnancy.

Or was this just hormones? Could she keep blaming her hormones for the swirling mess of confusion she felt when she looked at Micha?

Liar.

What?

Liar. You know it's not so confused any more.

She let the silk shirt fall from her hands. No, she couldn't lie to herself any more. She wasn't confused about how she felt about him. It was as if the closer she drew to him, he was becoming clearer and clearer, a lens adjusting until he was in focus.

Micha. The man who remembered where she'd always wanted to go. The man who, no matter what others had believed or how they had behaved, had never treated her business acumen with anything other than respect. Who had always stood up to the men in her family, honouring her grandfather's wishes, no matter what they were. The man who had set her on *fire* with a need so overwhelming and so incredible her body still reacted to just the thought of it. The man she had slept beside last night, who had given her everything she'd asked for. A man whose morals and character would make him the best father she could imagine for her child.

A soft knock on the door brought her out of her thoughts.

'There are drinks on the terrace for when you're ready,' Micha called through the door.

He had given her so much already. Could he give her even more? Could he give her the one thing she truly wanted? His heart?

Maria emerged from the bedroom suite just fifteen minutes later, dressed in a deep olive-green silk dress that floated down to her toes. After the flight, her ankles had felt a little swollen and she'd decided to leave her feet bare. The sleeveless dress draped down from shoulders and the dramatic V was perfect for her chest, which felt fuller than it had done before her pregnancy.

To the left of the secluded terrace was a small, but exquisite pool, brilliant white contrasting with rich deep blue tiles that made her heart happy to see. The terrace looked out over an incredible view—the slash of dusk touching the azure-blue horizon line of the sea was breathtaking. The mountains in the distance provided texture to the vista, and it wasn't that different to the Mediterranean view she loved so much. In fact, it reminded her of the little cottage she'd bought on Lake Trasimeno.

'You look beautiful, Maria.'

The words came from behind her and she let them settle about her before she turned to take him in. He, too, had changed from his travel clothes. The cream linen suit and pale blue shirt were about as relaxed as he permitted himself in the impeccable fashion he wore. And for the first time she wondered if they were the same in that. If they chose their clothes as armour against those who would take from them, or try to diminish them.

And suddenly she wanted to ask him. Ask him everything she'd been wondering about over the years. The little thoughts and questions she'd gathered and noted, that had become lists long enough to fill books.

'And you look very handsome,' she replied.

Micha blinked, the words reaching a part of him that he usually kept hidden. He wasn't stupid. He knew that he was attractive to most women, but handsome? From Maria? It felt like something shifted. He'd not been handsome to her back when they were younger—precisely because they had been younger. But they were adults now and everything was different in very small and very particular ways.

He gestured to the table set by the house staff, who had thankfully disappeared for the night. On pristine tablecloths had been placed a veritable feast of small plates containing food that looked incredible and smelled delicious. Only from the moment he'd spied Maria, his hunger for food had fled and been replaced by a desire that only she could satiate.

She came to the seat he held out for her and Micha caught the scent she wore, citrus, sweet, *soft*. That was what had surprised him about this Maria. The softness that didn't make her any less, but instead only made her seem *more*. More feminine, more powerful, more herself. As if she could finally be *all* the things that she wanted to be, rather than trying to force herself into the boxes that other people expected or needed from her.

'This looks wonderful,' she said appreciatively.

He had already removed any of the little plates that she couldn't have because of her pregnancy, and the chef had immediately presented him with a few alternatives. The plates were designed to be shared and he was happy to see her looking so eagerly at the food.

His mother had explained how ill she'd been with morning sickness. She hadn't had to say how useless his father had been at the time, and Micha had sworn that Maria would not be left to deal with anything like that on her own.

'There's so much here, I'm not sure we're going to eat even half of it,' she whispered.

There was a sweet, meaty tagine, stuffed fried sardines, *briwat*, the triangle pastries stuffed with cheese and meat, *zalook* with its stewed aubergine, tomatoes and spices, couscous and roasted vegetables, freshly cooked flatbreads and merguez sausages, and fresh tomato salads, with red onion and herbs.

'Eat whatever you want,' he said, placing a few things on her plate for her to start with, and then seeing to his own.

'You're still very considerate,' she said, her index finger running across the rim of the blue-and-white textured plate he'd just given her.

'I don't see why that would have changed,' he said with a small frown.

'You don't think that my family's obvious and inherent selfishness could have whittled that out of you, if you had been a man of lesser character? That working with them for so long wouldn't have rubbed off on you?' she asked, curious. 'Do you not think *I've* changed?' she asked, and instinctively he felt wary of where this was going.

He gave her question some thought.

'Yes, I think you did change. But it had nothing to do with the level of your character,' he said, finally raising his gaze to her. 'I think that your family gave you little choice. You were forced to fight for everything. But at least you know that you deserve everything you won.'

'You don't think you deserved what you have?'

'I would have absolutely none of this were it not for Gio,' he replied resolutely.

'I don't think that Gio is responsible for either your intelligence or your character.'

He clenched his jaw. 'I think that Gio's financial support gave me the luxury to be able to *use* my intelligence and maintain my character. There were many who grew up like me who didn't have that chance.'

Maria placed a hand on his forearm. 'I did not mean to start an argument, I just... I sometimes think that perhaps you don't give yourself enough credit for what you achieved. He may not have offered you the company first in his will, but he wouldn't have offered it at all if he didn't think you could run it.'

He reached for the pale yellow wine in the cooler to pour himself a glass, stopping just before he did so.

'Go ahead,' Maria said. 'You can have a glass. Don't feel you need not drink just because I can't.'

'Just the one,' he said, pouring a glass and taking a mouthful before responding to her statement. 'I was the stick. Antonio was the carrot. He always was.'

If Antonio had done what he'd said he'd do and divorce his inconvenient bride from England, if he'd married Maria, if Maria hadn't come to see him... If Gio had never sent him away all those years ago.

'I don't think Gio saw it that way. I certainly didn't,' Maria pressed on, unaware of the direction of his thoughts. But her statement pulled him right back to the present.

'How do you see me?' he asked, feeling suddenly more vulnerable and exposed than he'd ever felt in his life. He knew how he saw himself. He knew that he'd forced her into this marriage, knew that he'd ordered her around and neglected her the night of their wedding, but only because he couldn't stand the idea of being so close to her and not touching her. Last night had been torture to him. And for a while he thought he'd understood what she'd wanted from him. But now, when she was looking at him like she was, he wasn't sure whether it was her desire he saw, or his own wishful thinking.

Maria bit her lip. She felt it, the precipice they were standing at. She'd felt it in Paris, but that had been different. That had been fuelled by anger and hurt and a very determined, powerful kind of energy. This was different. Now, she felt...curious, tentative, hopeful, wanting, nervous, vulnerable, desperate not to be left again.

'How do I see you?' she said, repeating his question. And wanted to stop fighting the instinct to hold herself back. Hold her thoughts back, her feelings, in case they would be rejected and spurned, like her father always had, ignored like her mother always had, or not enough as she'd thought had been the case with him.

'I see you as powerful, as commanding, and proud,' she said, thinking of how he'd handled Peterson, who had notoriously cowed many members of her family. 'I see you as kind, as thoughtful,' she continued, thinking of his mother and the women in his life, which now included her. She remembered all the little things he'd done for her, opening her door, holding her chair, thoughtless things to him, but utterly foreign to some men out there. 'I see you as someone who is conscious of the impact of their actions and deeds,' she said, knowing that there were some out there who would have turned her away if they'd discovered her pregnancy. 'I see you as someone who is loyal.' She thought of the man who steadfastly clung to Gio's side long after he perhaps stopped deserving such fierce fealty. 'And I see the boy in you that I once loved.'

All of her experiences crowded into her mind and heart, jostling to remind her to be careful, to warn her against answering a question that was surely a trap. But she was so tired of fighting everyone else that she no longer had the energy or the inclination to fight herself.

'Do you think you could ever love the man?' Micha asked.

Her heart pounded in her chest.

'I think I could,' she lied. And it *was* a lie. Because, deep down, she knew that she *already* loved him. That perhaps she had never stopped.

He didn't move a muscle, but the golden glitter in his eyes exploded like fireworks. It was as if neither of them dared to breathe. And then slowly, ever so slowly, as if giving her every chance to stop him, to move away, to run, he stood from his chair and held his hand out for her to take.

This was the precipice. This was the moment. She would come back to this moment over the years, knowing how it had shaped her life, their lives. And she would never, ever regret what she did next.

She placed her hand in his and let him gently pull her to her feet. She was standing barely inches from him, close enough to feel the heat from his body, to see the little scar in his eyebrow, the mole on his cheek.

She was so caught up in her attention to him that she flinched when his hand cupped her cheek. He went to remove it, but she covered it with hers to keep it there. She leaned into the warmth of his palm, something in his touch that she'd never found anywhere else or in anyone else.

The scent of cedar, pepper and vanilla made her near dizzy with want for him. In Paris, she'd been almost out of her mind, out of her own body in some respects. Oh, she'd known what she was doing, but it felt as if she had been driven by the furies themselves.

This was different. This was slow, considered, grounded, rooted in something far deeper and stronger than the moment. She wasn't carried away—it wasn't thoughtless—but it was no less heady, no less intoxicating. If anything it felt *more*.

'Would you kiss me?' she asked.

Maria didn't know who was more surprised, Micha or herself.

But when the ghost of a smile traced his lips, she couldn't bring herself to regret it.

His gaze flicked between her mouth and her eyes, before he gently took her lips with his. It was a sampling. A tasting. A *testing*. And not even near enough to satiate her needs. Instead, it only inflamed her wants.

'Again?' she asked.

Once more, that ghost of a smile pulled at Micha's lips, but this time when he went to claim her mouth, she met him halfway, half open, and then, *then*, it happened.

That kiss that she'd only ever shared with him. The rush of *everything* she felt when he touched her. Tongues entwined, lips locked, her hand reached to his nape, gently fisting the hair gathered there, determined to hold him to her should he try to end the kiss that fed maddening amounts of magic into her blood.

His hand reached for her hip, fisting her dress in his palm, flexing and pulling her against him, her chest pressed to his, the muscles of his toned body, the growl in his throat travelling straight to her core as he began to lose that incredible control he had over himself.

'Again,' she sighed against his lips before he could even think of pulling away.

He pulled her against him and it wasn't enough to feel him between layers of clothes any more, just like it had never been enough to see him through layers of hurt and anger. She pulled at his shirt, tugging it from the waistband of his trousers, and he laughed a little and held her hand to stop her.

'Shall we take this inside? Can I finally find a bed to lay you on?'

The plea in his voice was as irrefutable as the want and need in his gaze, in his touch.

'God, yes, please,' she replied, and he picked her up in his arms and stalked through the villa and into a suite set for the perfect honeymoon.

CHAPTER ELEVEN

MICHA HOPED THAT Maria couldn't feel how his hands were shaking. *Shaking!* He wasn't some naive uncouth boy, but she made him feel like that, in the sense that she took him back through time, to how it *could* have been. *Would* have been if Gio hadn't sent him away and she'd not failed to come looking for him. He thrust those thoughts aside, ruthlessly. The past might have come to haunt him, but he couldn't bring that into this place. Not now, not here.

He laid Maria gently on the bed, her hair fanning out and around her shoulders, the olive-green silk dress cast in light and shade as it draped against the dips and hollows of her body, her breasts, her chest, her hips, her thighs… He couldn't stop looking. As if he couldn't quite believe she was here.

There'd been so much chaos in his mind in Paris, a little bit of confusion, a lot of surprise and a sense of completely overwhelming heady desire. But this? This felt different. This felt intentional, careful, considered and he was at peace with that. He was at peace with her. And that felt…more than it probably should.

Maria bit her lip, the nervous gesture bringing him back to the present. He didn't want her to feel a second's hesitation or doubt. Or was that actually true? Did he want her to think this through and still want to be here? With him? Wearing his ring? Carrying their child?

The thought melted the barriers he'd built around his heart, brick by brick in the days, weeks and months that had followed his first move to Paris all those years ago. As he'd waited for her to come to him. Because he could see now that they were here, she *had* eventually come to him. And that would have to be enough. Because he could no longer deny his feelings for her. Feelings that had never once gone away.

He picked up her hand and pressed a kiss to her palm, before coming to lie beside her on the bed, half content just to be there with her. He allowed himself the luxury of taking in the changes that the years had made. The lean lines her face had become, the startling light honeyed brown gaze watching him watch her.

'You have always been, and always will be, the most beautiful woman I ever know.'

Her mouth parted, as if in surprise at the softness of his words, but no sound came out. He gently pushed back a corkscrew curl from her forehead, and traced the curve of her cheek, the side of her neck, the hollow of her throat and across her collarbone.

Her body came alive beneath his, as if his touch were the strings of a puppeteer and he wanted to gather her to him and just *inhale* her. As if he could consume her, possess her, until they became one. He'd never wanted anyone like this. He'd been half terrified of his feelings eleven years ago, and was still half scared of them now. But he had to move past that fear if they were going to have any hope of the relationship he sometimes caught glimpses of in the deepest parts of his soul. A knowing of what they could be. Something so good and so pure, he wasn't sure he was worthy of it.

She looked at him then, something like sympathy in her gaze.

She raised her hand and mirrored the tour his fingers had taken, as she traced a fingertip over his hairline and skin. But her hand swept to his neck and pulled him towards her, and he swore he heard her whisper again, before his lips closed over hers.

He was hers to command.

Again and again and again he kissed her.

Chaste. Worshipful. Adoring. Enlightening.

Sighs not of surrender, but of yearning and want fell between them as he indulged them both, not in fast greedy grabs, but in easy, unhurried strokes and lingering tastes. Slowly, one by one, he unbuttoned her dress, slipping the silk tie around her waist and tossing it aside, even as it put erotic thoughts into his mind for the future. This, tonight, was something special. It was how that first time *should* have been between them.

He placed his hand over the silk of the skirt and stroked it up her legs, the satiny glide of the material over her smooth skin a delight to them both. Micha placed kisses to the stomach he bared to his gaze and touch and smiled as she squirmed in delight, breathy half laughs that were innocent and expectant, and lingering over the gentle swell of the child they had created together. Their eyes met as softness sank into something more. Something serious. As if they both knew how much this moment meant to the other, how important it was.

His hand rested over her abdomen, as her hand came up to cup his jaw, and he knew in that moment that he'd found it again. The heart he'd given her all those years ago, lost to him until now.

'Let me make love to you.'

To anyone else it would sound arrogant, commanding. But he knew she'd understand it as a request, because she was the one who held all the power in this moment.

'Please,' she replied, and he dropped his head in relief and thanks, before slipping his hands beneath her to gather her to him. He buried his head in her, inhaling her scent, giving himself to her as she wrapped her arms around him, holding him to her. And in that instant, he surrendered to her and she let him. She took everything that he offered, unquestioning and without judgement.

His lips found her chest, her breasts, her mouth, her shoulder, his hands finding her hips, her curves, palming firm muscles and lithe grace, until they were both panting and desperate.

He released her only to reach towards the nightstand, when she stayed his hand. He looked at her questioningly.

'We don't need to use protection,' she said, her voice husky, eyes sparkling.

'Are you sure?' he hesitated.

She smiled, shyly. 'Yes.'

'I've been tested. You have nothing to worry about.'

'I know you would never put me at risk,' she said with a solemn gaze, before pulling him back to her and into a kiss that reached his very soul. The trust she was giving him, letting him into her in such a way, humbled him.

Maria looked into his gaze, so serious it was as if he were almost sad. And she felt it. A kind of grief for all they had been through, all the hurts and the years apart, all the painful ways they had been thrust into adulthood, the innocence that had once been between them long since lost.

She kissed him in a way hoping to heal, in a way that promised to do better, be better, for him, for their child, for herself. A kiss that started off slow, reverent, but stoked the fires of need until flames licked at her skin where he touched her. Restless with need, her legs shifted to make room for him, as he pressed open-mouthed kisses to her collarbone, her chest, as he palmed her breast and nipped at her nipple, licking, stroking, urging those flames higher.

Damp heat pooled between her legs, pulse points throbbing incessantly, needing his touch or tongue to soothe them. Need became sighs that fell from her lips, as her body undulated against him, desperate for friction, for release, for *him*.

'I could watch you forever,' he said, his gaze on hers as he parted her thighs with one hand, his fingers delving between her legs and finding her core. Her back arched away from the bed as he tested her readiness with his fingers, his thumb pressing gently, but firmly against her clitoris.

'Move for me?' he all but begged, and she understood that he wanted her to move against his thumb. That he wanted her to please herself. Heart thumping wildly in her chest, emotion thick in her throat, her entire body flushed, nipples tightening under his voyeurism as she moved against his hand, the moan of pleasure filling the air between them; hers, his, it didn't matter.

'Micha,' she begged.

'Not yet.'

'But I want you with me,' she all but pleaded.

'But I want this more,' he replied, forcing her to a pleasure that was near indecent.

Her gasps filled the room, the rose petals crushed beneath her, and his other hand came to rest across her abdomen, comforting, protective. Red slashes appeared on his cheeks as she drew closer and closer to an orgasm she half feared.

'Micha.'

Her hands reached for his, needing that connection, that anchor, as if without it she might just fly away and lose herself completely. The orgasm built with a kind of slow intensity she'd never experienced, with a tide that started at her feet, creeping higher and higher up her body until she crested a wave so big she thought she might drown beneath the pleasure he brought her.

Her entire self was lost, boneless, weightless, thoughtless, lost not to nothingness but to him. Micha. Who held her and soothed her as she came back to herself in shivers and lightning strikes that threatened to change the very fabric of her being.

She opened her eyes to find his gaze on hers, wonder in his eyes...the same wonder that she felt. *Micha*. It was the gaze of a boy she'd not seen for eleven years and ridiculously she felt tears well in her eyes, and blinked, hoping to stop the flow before it started.

'*Mi amore*,' he said, but she wasn't ready. Wasn't ready to hear the rest of what he had to say. She felt so raw and vulnerable, she knew instinctively that he could break her, not with savage words or rejection, but with his love.

She took his hand and pressed a kiss to his palm. Used that same hand to draw him to her, and kissed away the hurt and the fear that she felt, willingly losing herself to him and his body. And if he knew what she was doing, he had the kindness not to stop her.

She moaned when she felt the steel-like press of his erection against her thigh. Ravenous and wanton, that's what he'd turned her into. She reached for him, palming the velvet length of him, her thumb tracing the small liquid bead at the head of his penis, and bit her lip in delicious expectation. He batted away her hand, and she growled in playful frustration. And when his lips found hers, she could trace the half smile on his mouth.

'Micha,' she whispered into his ear, letting her sighs tell him how much she wanted him. How much she wanted this.

He notched himself at her core, kissing her deeply. She felt the racing of his heart against hers, where their chests pressed against each other and it was as he whispered '*mi amore*' into her ear that he pushed into her slowly, surrounding her in such exquisite pleasure she wasn't sure where he ended and she began. Time lost all meaning as slow thrusts turned quick, powerful and deliciously hard. He filled her completely and left her almost never, as they spent hours and seconds and minutes discovering what it should have always been like between them. By the time another orgasm came for her, Micha was with her and when she fell, she was wrapped in his arms and they fell together.

Micha watched Maria sleep. She was completely still. No movement at all. Her head was on his outstretched arm and he didn't care that he was getting pins and needles. He wouldn't move her for the world. She was so peaceful like this. None of the energy that forced her so determinedly through the day. It was fascinating.

'Why are you staring at me?' she whispered, with her eyes still closed, and he jerked back a tiny bit in shock.

With a smile on her face she turned in to him, nuzzling closer, and his heart nearly careened right out of his chest.

'Don't stop,' she whispered, making herself comfortable. 'I like it.' And with that she went straight back to sleep and he held her like that all the way until the morning.

Over the next couple of days, Micha wondered whether he was living in a dream. Every morning, they would have breakfast out on the beautiful sun-drenched patio. The sounds of birds and the sight of the sea were an accompaniment to freshly squeezed orange juice, mint tea, his espresso—of course—*halwa dyal kouk*, a type of coconut cake that Maria couldn't get enough of, bread, olive oil, honey and other pastries filled with the flavours of orange and almond. The heat from the sunrise—Maria was an unconscionably early riser—was delicious. It crept slowly and seduced, relaxing muscles and sinking into weary bones. He tried to remember the last time he'd had a break like this. A holiday.

Never.

He'd been working so long and so hard, trying to outrun the poverty he'd grown up with and the insecurity he'd lived with daily.

After breakfast, Maria would speak to one of the house staff and they would be whisked away on a magical mystery tour. On the first day, they'd visited Medersa Ben Yousef, the fourteenth-century religious school that was full of the *zellij* tiling that he was beginning to really like, ancient cedar wood ceilings and breathtaking stucco work. On the second day they visited Souk Semmarine, where Maria deftly handled negotiations with several store owners to acquire intricately detailed carpets and cut-brass lanterns. The leather work was impeccable and she bought a wallet for Antonio, and Enzo—her newly acquainted cousin—and bracelets for Ivy and Erin, their wives. And when she smiled at him and asked if there was something he wanted to buy, he just shook his head and smiled. Because there, in the middle of a market in Marrakesh, with the scents wafting over him from the *ahba kedima*, the spice market, and the smell of coals, and hot leather from the *haddadine*, the blacksmith's alley, it hit Micha hard.

He had everything he needed. Everything he'd *ever* wanted.

And if there was a thought in the back of his head, an alarm bell, that warned him it was too good to be true, then he ignored it.

On the third day, Maria took him to the Yves Saint Laurent Museum and the Jardin Majorelle, where he lived, where even Micha was awed by the incredible collection of art within such a beautiful setting. The design of the building was heavily formed by contrasting straight and curved lines, and radically different to where Saint Laurent had lived, where powerful colours sat perfectly with Moroccan architecture, and it made Micha realise that he'd not really thought of his home in such a way. But seeing Maria draw in all the colour, the inspiration, the architecture, seeing her come alive, he realised he wanted her to feel the same way about where they would live. He wanted to create that for her.

And at night? Well, never in his wildest dreams had he imagined anything so incredible. They spent hours rediscovering themselves and each other. He placed kisses on her belly, where their child was growing each day, and each night he slept with his hand possessively and comfortingly placed over them.

Maria beckoned him over from where she was bent at the waist, looking at a tray of jewellery that could cost less than their breakfast. He'd realised that for Maria, it wasn't the cost that mattered, but how beautiful she found it. She'd just as easily wear a dress from the market as one of YSL's haute couture pieces. As long as something about it caught her eye.

'What do you think of this?'

'I think you like it and that's all I need to know,' he replied, but cast a gaze over the handmade silver necklace. Rows and rows of tiny little beads, that rich blue of lapis lazuli. It *was* beautiful.

'Wise man,' the store owner said with a smile.

Micha inclined his head in recognition of the high praise. Maria slapped him playfully on the arm.

'Do you *like* it?' she pressed.

'Am I the one who will be wearing it?' he toyed.

'Yes. That and nothing else. In bed. All night long,' she replied, deadpan, and the store owner coughed in shock and Micha threw his head back and laughed.

By the time he stopped, he realised that she was looking at him in a strange way, and after buying the necklace he most definitely would *not* be wearing, they found a shaded table at an out-of-the-way cafe for Maria to rest the ankles that were, as predicted, getting a little swollen.

After ordering their drinks, a mint tea for her and an espresso for him, he asked her about it.

'It's just...been a while since I heard you laugh like

that. Even when we were younger, you were always so serious.'

'And you were always trying to make me laugh,' he replied, the smile on his lips evident in his tone.

And then you weren't there to make me laugh.

'It's nice. I like it.'

'What?'

'Your laugh. It's nice. You should laugh more.'

'I will do whatever brings you joy,' he said, the words out of his mouth before he realised how vulnerable that could make him. But when he saw the look in her eyes, he couldn't bring himself to regret them. She looked as if he'd given her a gift far more precious than any stone, diamond or jewel in the whole of Marrakesh.

Is this what we could have? Is this what it could be like?

The question was in her gaze, so strong, so powerful, so in tune with what he was thinking that he wondered if it were even possible.

And, of course, *that* was when the universe decided to answer.

Maria's phone vibrated in her purse, the sound on silent. She wanted to ignore it. Unwilling to break the moment between them. It was so precious, these glimpses of what things could be like between them. Almost like when they had been younger, but better somehow. More mature.

But the phone didn't stop ringing, so she checked the screen and her heart thudded painfully in her chest.

Papa.

He never called. Which was why she knew, instinctively, whatever he was calling about couldn't be good.

She smiled up at Micha.

'Excuse me for a moment?'

'Of course,' he said, as she stood up and made her way towards the bathroom she knew Micha had believed had been her intended destination.

Out of sight from the table, she pulled the phone from her bag and answered.

'What do you want?' she asked without preamble.

'You need to come back,' her father commanded.

'Why?' she asked, instead of saying *No. It's my honeymoon, I don't want—*

'We're calling a no-confidence vote against Rufina.'

'What?' she asked, her world seesawing, as her mind scrabbled to keep up. 'We' being the family, the *board*. Any one of whom could call such a vote.

They were trying to oust Micha.

'Tomorrow. Be there. And if you vote with *us*, when he's gone we'll vote you in.'

The buzzing in her ears wasn't enough to drown out what her father was saying.

'He's my husband, Papa.'

'He's a trumped-up street thug who got my daughter pregnant and will ruin this company.'

'But we got Peterson on board,' she tried to explain.

'The paperwork hasn't been filed yet. That's why the vote is tomorrow.'

'Papa, this isn't right.'

'It doesn't have to be right. The company should be run by a Gallo. That Rufina is at the helm is unacceptable.'

'But I am?' she asked. 'Acceptable?'

'You're better than *him*,' her father spat. 'So, get back

here for then, and cast your vote with us and we'll put you in as CEO.'

Maria clenched her jaw.

'It's everything you ever wanted,' her father dangled. 'Gallo Group will be yours.'

Maria stared unseeing at the cafe wall for long after the call ended.

What should she do? She had to tell him about the vote, but…

We'll put you in as CEO.

She started when Micha placed his hand on her arm.

'Is everything okay?' he asked, concern clear in his gaze.

'No, I don't think it is.'

Micha remained tight-lipped on the car journey back to the villa as she told him that a vote of no confidence was being called tomorrow.

He said nothing to her. Absolutely nothing. But he called his assistant to make arrangements for the jet to meet them at the airport and take them back to Rome immediately. She looked across the car to where Micha sat, grim faced and lock jawed staring out of the window. If she told him about her father's offer, it would only make things worse.

The car drew up to the villa and he got out, and although he came round to her side of the car, and held the door open for her, his gaze roamed everywhere but on her.

She wanted to know what he was thinking. What he was feeling. And for the first time in her life, she *hated* Gallo Group. Hated what it did to her family. Hated how it made everyone and everything around her so desperate and selfish.

How it made *her* feel desperate and selfish.

Because she couldn't deny that a part of her saw how much she wanted it. For years it was all she'd wanted. The company. To show what she could do. To prove herself, to her family. To her father. To Gio. To *herself*.

But at what cost?

She followed Micha into the villa, and through to the living room, disconcerted when Micha turned to stare at her intently.

'What?' she asked.

'Did your father say anything else? When he told you about the no-confidence vote?'

Maria paused, her heart throbbing painfully in her chest.

'No,' she lied.

And then she saw it. The knowledge. The betrayal. And she wished to god that she could call her words back.

He shook his head, and turned away from her in disgust.

'Micha—'

'Do you really believe I'm so stupid as to not realise what he's offered you in exchange for your vote against me? There is no one in the company even remotely suitable for the president and CEO seat other than you. He's offered you the role.'

'And you think I'll take it? You think I'd choose *that* over *you*?' she demanded outraged.

'Of course I do! You did then.'

'What are you talking about?' Maria asked, confusion blooming in her heart and head.

'Eleven years ago, the day Gio told me he was sending me to Paris. When I came to see you. We were on the lawn, remember?'

No, she didn't remember. All she remembered was the shock and hurt of confusion. The agony that had threatened to swallow her whole after he'd left without a word. She—

I have to ask you something.

The smell of grass and the feel of the sun on her skin.

What would you do to become head of this company? If Gio offered it to you?

Anything. You know that.

Her stomach dropped, plummeting to the ground.

She stared up at him in confusion.

'You asked me that, without telling me what was going on?' she demanded, feeling a rush of anger. 'You asked me…without giving me the context,' she said slowly, realising what he'd done. 'You set me up to fail. Because there was no way I could answer that question properly without understanding why you were asking it! You didn't trust me. You didn't trust my feelings for you,' she threw at him, her heart breaking.

It hadn't been her. All this time, it wasn't something she'd done. It had been him. He'd always have left. Because he didn't trust her. He didn't think he was worthy of her.

'You've wanted this company almost since before you could walk. All you did was tell me the truth. You should take their offer,' Micha said, breaking her heart. 'It's what you've always wanted.'

'You,' she confessed, her throat raw around the word. 'You were what I always wanted. From the very beginning. You are the only man I have ever wanted and…you are the only man I've ever been with.'

Standing so close, she could see the impact her words had on him. The realisation that she had been a virgin in Paris. His cheeks flushed and his eyes widened. He opened his mouth as if to speak, but she didn't want to hear it. *Couldn't.*

'But if you'd told me back then,' she pressed on, 'if you'd *trusted* me, trusted my feelings for you, if you'd explained what you were really asking me, then I would have answered differently. But you didn't. You didn't trust me then and you still don't trust me now. *That's* why you left me. It wasn't because I chose them, that's just an excuse,' she said, repeating Antonio's accusation from the night before the wedding. 'One you've hidden behind for years.'

At her words, he shut down. As if all feeling had been shoved behind an impenetrable door.

'That's the way you see it? That I abandoned you?' he asked, his tone horribly level compared to the agony in hers.

'Yes!'

'And what did you do?'

'Nothing!' she cried, unable to call back the hurt that was spilling out of her. Why was he being so cruel? So harsh? So unfeeling!

'Exactly.'

Wait, what?

She stared at him in confusion.

'Maria, you have fought for absolutely everything in your life. You fought schoolyard bullies, you stood up to your grandfather before your uncles could even think to do such a thing. You worked harder and more determinedly at work, pushing back every single time they tried to discriminate and intimidate you.'

'Yes, I did,' she said with pride, as the distance between them grew smaller and smaller.

He was almost within touching distance now, her heart pounding in her chest, blood rushing in her ears. This argument had been brewing between them for *years* and it was finally here. *He* was finally here. His gaze was stormy, his breath seeming to punch the air between them. He was angry, she realised. Angrier than she'd ever seen him. This was nothing like the back-and-forth they'd had in Paris, where no matter how cutting or cruel, his impartiality had held him in check. But that was gone now. Here was the wild energy he'd had about him when he'd been younger. The passion that had drawn her, the drive.

He raised his hand to gently sweep aside a curling tendril from her face and tuck it behind her ear, the careful gesture seeming painfully at odds with the tension in the room.

'You fight everything Maria. So why didn't you fight for us?'

His words were a whisper, with the power of an atomic bomb.

The shock wave cut straight through her, through the years, through the hurts, through the feelings and agonies she'd experienced to the heart of something they'd never dared confront. The devastation of it was made somehow worse by the fact his words weren't a shout, weren't a ferocious demand, as if he had long ago surrendered to the belief that he wasn't worthy of such a thing. As if he'd already given up before she'd begun to see.

To see the part that she played in the past.

He searched her face as if finally, after eleven years,

he saw what he needed to. The dawning realisation of what she had done.

Or not done.

'Why didn't you fight for me, Maria?' he asked.

Her soul shivered beneath his question. The truth emerging from the deepest, most sacred part of her childhood hurts. He deserved the truth as much as she deserved to say it.

'Because if I failed, if you still walked away, there would have been nothing left of me,' she confessed, her heart shattering into a thousand pieces.

He stared at her, as if understanding her pain, but that it didn't change a thing.

'So, who didn't trust who, Maria?'

Tears welled in her eyes, threatening to fall. Too much hurt and too much pain shimmered between them. He hadn't trusted her to love her, and she hadn't fought to prove that she did, because she'd been scared too. Hurt by his rejection of her, she'd built a steel wall around her so that nothing and no one could hurt her like that again. But if she'd tried…if she had reached out to him…

'I—'

'The car will take you to the airport,' he said interrupting her, ending the conversation.

'And what about you?'

'I need some time to think. I'll see you at the meeting.'

And with that, he stalked out of the room, but to Maria it felt as if he was stalking out of her life. Again.

CHAPTER TWELVE

KARL, HER DRIVER whenever she was in Rome, eyed her warily in the car's rear-view mirror.

'Shouldn't you be going in there, Ms G—I mean, Mrs—'

'Not yet,' Maria said, staring at the entrance to the Gallo Group Headquarters in Rome, through the blacked-out window of the town car.

She was watching them all arrive. Several generations of Gallo men, all dressed in impeccably tailored dark suits, with crisp white shirts and pinned ties. The family resemblance imprinted on similarly dark features.

Her phone vibrated with a message from Antonio.

I'm two minutes out.

She'd called him from the plane late last night, pouring her heart out to him in a way that she'd not been able to with Micha. Oh, she'd wanted to, but she hadn't trusted herself that night. She'd been too hurt. Too confused. Too…ashamed.

Antonio had threatened to get in the car and drive to her right then and there, but Maria wasn't even going to get into Italy for another four hours, so there'd have been no point. She'd wanted to know, needed to know, whether what Micha had said was right.

Antonio's voice had been regretful.

'I'd always known that it would have been hard for Micha to say no to Gio. And if Gio knew about you and Micha, of course he would have sent him away. And I...'

'What?'

'Well, I was so angry at how he'd hurt you, I refused to reach out to him.' The shame in her cousin's voice matched the one she felt in her heart.

'You think he's right then?' she asked, not because she needed him to tell her. She knew that Micha was right. 'That I...didn't fight for him?'

'I think we were all young. And,' he said hesitantly, 'I think you were hurt and trying to protect yourself. But I also don't think that he's entirely wrong, Maria. I'm not sure that, even with all the information available, you'd have been *able* to choose Micha. Yes, you were a fighter, even back then, but Maria...you were seventeen. Your father would have disowned you, Gio would have had to fire Micha, he would have lost every bit of financial security he had. It would have been...'

'Impossible,' Maria finished when Antonio trailed off.

Maria had looked out of the plane window, just as she was doing now from the car. It hurt to even think that she would have chosen the company back then. It seemed inconceivable, but realistically, could she have?

'Do you think Gio knew that? Do you think that's why Gio sent him away?' she had asked Antonio.

'If you're asking me whether Gio was somehow doing all this out of the kindness of his own heart? I can't tell you that. He was a very manipulative, business-focused, difficult man. But speak to Enzo about it one day, he might have a different story to tell.'

She watched the last members of the board enter the building and held her breath. She realised that she was waiting for Micha. But she hadn't seen him since she arrived, and didn't know if he had got here before her.

Her door opened and her cousin smiled down at her with a familiar grin.

'So. Are you ready to fight the family, Maria?' Antonio asked.

'I am ready to fight *for* my family,' she replied, taking his hand and stepping out of the car.

She should have felt a little bad about turning up at her favourite designer's studio last night at 11:00 p.m. Instead of going home from the airport, she'd called from the plane and explained what she wanted. Her friend had not disappointed.

She had on a black suit, with a few small adjustments. Instead of trying to diminish the way that her baby had increased in size, the tailored pantsuit fit her perfectly to show off her pregnancy. The waist rose a little higher than normal in order, almost, to proclaim it to the world. The white tucked-in shirt and loose tie made her look effortlessly cool and chic. And her black Louboutins made her feel powerful.

She was done hiding.

She and Antonio entered the lift that would take them to the boardroom, and he respected her need for silence as she gathered herself, preparing to give the speech that she'd spent all night on. She hadn't had much sleep, but she didn't need it. She was running on adrenaline and need. The need to do what she should have done eleven years ago.

When they arrived, they were ushered into the boardroom where around a table that sat twenty-four, only two chairs remained empty. Micha sat at the head of the table, his face utterly impassive, hiding his every thought from her.

While the gazes of her family ping-ponged between them, Antonio gestured her towards the seat at the direct opposite end of the table to her husband.

Antonio slipped into the seat beside her and she forced herself to take in, one by one, the faces of the men around the table. She felt Micha's gaze on her, but she needed to do this first.

Her uncles, her cousins, their sons. Three generations of Gallos and she was the only woman.

She saw expectation on their faces. A little resentment. But a huge amount of satisfaction. As if they'd all been waiting for this from the very moment of her grandfather's last breath. They were vultures and she hated every single one of them.

Her gaze rested on her father, who sat to her right. The man for whom neither she nor her mother had ever been good enough to capture his interest or attention, until now.

We'll put you in as CEO.

And he'd thought that would make her fall in line.

He hadn't ever really seen her, had he? He'd never realised what she had become in spite of him. Powerful, strong, dynamic and damn good at her job. She was so much more than just his daughter. She was a businesswoman. A wife. And a mother.

And it was time to protect her family.

'We are here to cast a vote of confidence for or against the current CEO of Gallo Group,' her father said to absolutely no one's surprise. 'I don't see a reason to delay. I shall start the vote. No confidence,' he said.

And one by one, up the length of the table, votes were cast.

No confidence, no confidence, no confidence.

And through every single vote, Maria held the gaze that Micha had locked on her. His expression, almost one of boredom and unchanging, until Antonio's vote.

Full confidence.

Micha didn't lift his eyes from hers, but he did blink. He hadn't expected that, Maria realised with a spike of sadness for the friendship they'd once had. For the Three Musketeers that they'd once been.

But then it was her turn and every single set of eyes in the room looked to her in rabid expectation.

From a very young age, Micha had become adept at hiding his feelings and he doubted that anyone around the table would see anything more than a kind of lazy boredom. But beneath that outward display, was seething, gut-wrenching tension.

From the moment she'd left for the airport, he'd been reeling. For years he'd clung to the belief that she'd have done anything for Gallo Group. That she'd always have chosen it over him. But he realised in the silence left by her absence, that she'd been right. He *hadn't* given her a choice. Not really. He'd not had the confidence to trust that she'd pick him, and selectively he had chosen to frame that choice in a way that had set her up to fail.

Because then and even now, he'd not really ever felt that she'd pick him. And no, she hadn't fought for him, but he hadn't fought for her either. He'd surrendered to his fears and she'd deserved better than that.

Now, his eyes locked on the woman he'd given his heart away to more than eleven years ago and wished he could go back in time to fix it.

'Maria?' her father said. 'As CFO, how do you vote?'

'With my family,' she replied, and his heart flatlined.

From the corner of his eye, Micha saw the sickening smirk on her father's face. He opened his mouth to say something, but Maria cut him off.

'With Micha Rufina. My husband, the father of my child and the best CEO Gallo Group could have after Gio. With Micha Rufina,' she repeated before adding, 'the man I love.'

Gasps of shock and cries of frustration echoed out across the table at the same time as his heart soared back to life. He felt the pump of blood round his entire body and he would have sworn on a Bible that he'd heard his blood whoosh in his veins.

She loved him.

Beneath the table he fisted his hands to stop himself from sweeping everything aside and rushing over to her to take in his arms.

She could have had it. She could have had the whole of Gallo Group. She'd have been CEO. And she'd chosen him. As his brain tried to catch up to the instinctive reaction of his heart, Maria turned to look at the members of the board.

'None of you, not a single one, has brought in the revenue that Micha has over the last eleven years. He turned

Paris around from a middle-of-the-road satellite post to the second-highest revenue earner to Rome. I don't know what poison my father has been dripping into your ears, but surely, *surely*, none of you would do anything as monumentally stupid as to remove the man who has consistently built and improved processes and revenue in ways that only financially benefit you?

'I mean, what would lack *more* confidence than making a decision that negatively impacted the price of your shares and your income?' she said, turning on her father. 'It almost reeks of sabotage, to make such a risky move when Gallo Group is still on such shaky ground following Gio's death. I mean…of course, if that *were* the case,' she said, her tone heavy on implication, just as Micha realised where she was going with this, 'then when all your shares dropped so shockingly low, there would really only be one person in this room with enough money to buy them off you before you lost any more money. And how very kind that person would be. To buy all of your shares from you,' she said, her tone turning whip sharp, 'at a knock-down price, in order to have complete ownership of Gallo Group.'

One by one, he watched the confused faces of Gallo Group's board realise what Maria was implying: that her father was purposefully sabotaging GG in order to engineer a buyout leaving him as the sole owner. And whether or not it was the truth, whether that had been his intention all along—which Micha believed probably was the case—Maria had just successfully managed to turn every single selfish one of them against him.

The shock and fury on the faces of the board rivalled only what he'd seen when they had been told that *he* would be the one stepping into the CEO position and he almost felt sorry for them. Almost.

And then he couldn't help himself. He laughed. Because in that moment, Maria really had shown herself to be worthy of running Gallo Group.

He stared at his wife. The pride, the joy, the genuine love he felt for her poured into his gaze and when she caught it, he thought that she'd understood. The flare of her eyes, the flush on her cheeks, the little hitch in her chest as her breath caught. He was almost sure that she'd felt his very thoughts.

'So,' Maria said, turning back to the faces around the table. 'Would you like to try this again? All in favour?'

One after the other, they raised their hands to cast their votes again, her father looking absolutely thunderous, his face an angry blotchy red.

Micha didn't spare a single person a second glance, even as they all voted in favour of him this time, with the sole exclusion of Maria's father, who desperately stuck to his guns. Micha didn't care. He didn't once take his eyes off Maria, not even as the rest of the board members filed out of the room, under harsh whispers and grumbles, utterly deflated and more than a little angry.

Throughout it all, he took in how glorious she was, truly in her element, finally taking her position, whether in title or not, as head of the Gallo family. He wondered whether this was what Gio had been hoping for, or whether the old man would be turning in his grave. Micha liked to think that, somehow, he'd always known that this was the way it would be.

That if they could get over the deep hurts holding them back when they'd been younger, that *this* was how incredible it could be between him and Maria. That only through the trials and tribulations they'd been through in their time apart had they become strong enough to reach for what they wanted. Each other.

She dropped his gaze, only to speak in hushed tones to Antonio, who glanced in Micha's direction, eyes narrowed in assessment, before turning back to Maria, nodding and leaving the room. Maria closed the door behind him.

She turned to lean back against the door.

And for a moment they remained like that, staring at each other across the boardroom.

'Did you know?' she asked him.

He didn't bother pretending not to understand her. 'I had my suspicions that this was what your father was after. When did you realise that's what he was doing?'

She bit her lip. 'Last night. After speaking to Antonio. Enzo had given him a heads-up that my father had approached him for his vote. Enzo's position on the board might be new, but despite all accounts of him being some scandalous playboy, he is, in fact, a very shrewd businessman and was quick to realise what was going on.'

'He wasn't here today?'

'He couldn't come on such short notice, but he'd given permission for Antonio to vote for him in favour of you.'

It felt a little unusual to have the support of a stranger, but although no one had known Enzo Rossetti that long, Maria's cousin seemed to have become a close friend to Antonio and Maria.

Maria closed the distance between them with a step.

'I didn't know,' he said, needing her to understand.

'I didn't know, in Paris, that you'd never been with anyone.'

'I wouldn't change a single thing about it,' Maria replied, truthfully, defiantly, her hand protecting her stomach.

'Maria, you deserved—'

'I wouldn't change a single thing,' she said again. 'It was perfect, it was us. It was the beginning of us,' she said, reaching for his hand as if unable to hold herself back from touching him.

'You are incredible,' Micha said, unashamed to offer his praise of her. No matter what happened between them now, not after their last exchange back in Morocco, he wanted her to know that. 'And I will happily step down as president and CEO,' he said honestly and truly. Nothing was worth more to him than her. Nothing. Not a job, not a company and certainly not his ego. He wanted her, in whatever way he could get her. Nothing else mattered.

The man I love.

She looked at him, and for a moment, he was reminded of how this all started, back in Paris, in a different headquarters.

'I don't want it,' she replied easily.

'What? I—'

'No,' she said, interrupting him. 'I don't want it. I thought I did. I thought it would finally give me the acceptance I've been craving for an entire lifetime. That it would give me security and recognition. I thought that perhaps if I was CEO, finally, I'd be worthy of my father's attention. But I realised that being CEO wouldn't give me any of that. And I don't want to be the kind of person that would do what he wanted me to do to get there.

'The only person that accepted me for who I was, was you,' she said, closing the distance between them. 'The only person that ever made me feel loved was you,' she said, tears adding a sheen to her eyes that stole his breath, and yanked on his heart. 'The only person I ever loved was you.'

Her words were like a puzzle piece, finally slotting into place after eleven years, like a thick heavy chain that had encased his heart, falling away and letting him breathe, letting his heart beat, true and strong for the first time in *forever*.

'You, Micha Rufina. I love you. You are all I ever wanted, and all I will ever need,' she said, looking up at him with the kind of love he thought he'd never see again in his lifetime.

'I love you,' she whispered again as she rose onto her tiptoes to press her lips gently, chastely, perfectly against his.

Maria wanted to give him this. She wanted him to know, whether he loved her or not, no matter what happened between them, she needed him to know that she loved him. That she'd fought for him and that she would always fight for him. Not because he was her husband, or because he was the father of her child, but because he deserved it.

She lowered back down onto her feet, staring up at him with all the hope in her chest and the love in her heart. She didn't need anything from him, but she needed him to understand that.

'You humble me, Maria,' he said, the emotion in the depths of his gaze filling her up, nearly consuming her whole. 'I am in awe of you. I am truly sorry that your family didn't see in you what I did. The amazing, incredible, talented, powerful, dynamic, quick-witted and strong-hearted woman you have become. I am lucky just to get to love you,' he whispered, as if shocked by the truth of his own words.

His hand came to cup her cheek and she couldn't help but lean into his palm. The safety he had always offered her, the protection.

'You are my family, Micha. And our child. That is all I'll ever need,' she vowed, the words more binding than their marriage certificate.

'I think Antonio might have something to say about that,' Micha teased and she smiled, and pressed a kiss against the palm of his hand, before turning back to look up at him.

'I love you,' he said, this time with no trace of tease or humour. His love was serious, grounded, a decade in the making, just as hers was. It was serious in a way that only those who had known what it was to be unloved could feel. Serious in the tears that rose to press against the backs of her eyes as something in her shifted, healed and became new and fresh and precious.

He kissed her then, the first of many that had no questions, only answers, only security, only love.

'What do we do now?' she asked, against his lips.

'Well, right now, I'm taking my wife back to my apartment and making love to her all night long.'

'Lucky wife,' she replied with a smile.

'Lucky husband,' he said, smiling down at her, the flames of his desire flickering in his gaze.

'And then?' Maria asked.

'Well, then we get to spend the rest of our lives together, happily...'

'Ever...' she added.

'After,' he concluded with a kiss that they both remembered for many years to come.

EPILOGUE

THE SUN SHONE down on the garden and glinted off the clear flat surface of Lake Trasimeno beyond. Micha's sunglasses would have shaded his gaze, but his eyes were closed, and he was content to listen to the sounds around him. The breeze playing in the leaves of the trees and the birds calling to each other, nothing but the sounds of summer and serene—

'Elletra Valentina Rufina Gallo, I swear to god, if you don't come back here and clean up your mess, I will ground you for the rest of the summer.'

His wife's angry voice travelled out of the villa and down to where he was in the garden.

'Mama! That is *not* fair,' replied their daughter, just as angry. It probably shouldn't have come as a surprise that she had become as much of a fighter as her mother. And while neither parent would have it any other way, it had made—and would continue to make—things both interesting and *loud*.

'Papa,' Emilio whispered.

'*Si?*' Micha whispered back.

'Should I go and help?' Emilio asked. Their fourteen-year-old son was the softest of all of them, so earnest and so quiet, it sometimes made Micha ache just to watch how careful he was with other people.

'No, that's not necessary. It's Elletra's mess and she needs to clean it up,' Micha replied, not unkindly, but firmly.

'But I don't want her to be grounded all summer. And the others will be here soon,' he said, his voice concerned.

'Is she really going to be grounded?' Elisabetta, their youngest at twelve, piped up from behind Micha where she was making daisy chains.

Micha turned to take in the light halo of rich curls on her head.

'Not if she cleans her room,' he said, reaching to sweep her up into his arms and tickle her sides, sending her into a riot of giggles as Emilio looked on, wanting to join in, but struggling with being the young man he was feeling his way into. Micha pulled him into the fray and the three of them were a jumble of limbs and laughs and kisses.

'You started without me,' Maria complained as she collapsed onto the ground to join them, Elisabetta climbing from Micha onto her mother, her long limbs angular and pointy as Micha took an elbow to the gut that made both Maria and Emilio laugh.

'Where's Elletra?' Elisabetta asked.

'Tidying her room,' Maria growled gently.

Emilio rolled away and Micha propped himself up on one arm, taking in his beautiful wife. Not one day had gone by where he hadn't realised how lucky he was. They'd spent too much time apart, he'd missed out on too much and he'd vowed that he would never miss another moment as long as they lived. He loved her with the kind of adoration that he thought might have lessened with time, but instead it had only grown.

'Don't look at me like that in front of the kids,' Maria whispered as she planted a frustratingly chaste kiss against his lips.

'Why not?' he asked. 'I want another.'

Maria's eyes widened with shock, her gasp a punch of air against his mouth.

'What?' Maria said, becoming very still.

'Yes, Antonio and Ivy have four, Erin and Enzo also have four. We need another.'

'It's not a competition, Micha,' she said, slapping him on the arm.

'I know that. I just... I want four,' he said with a careless shrug.

'Our first just put three more grey hairs on my head. Are you sure you want another? Now?' Maria demanded.

'You're so sexy when you're pregnant, *mi amore*,' he whispered, reaching his hand out to stroke across her stomach.

'Sweet talk will get you nowhere, Micha,' she warned.

The sound of a car on the gravel drive at the front of the house made the kids scatter, running full pelt to greet their cousins. Whether it was Enzo's brood or Antonio's, it didn't matter. The cousins ranging in age from six to sixteen had nicknamed themselves the Musketeers.

'Okay. How about *dirty* talk?' he asked, cutting off the squeal of her laughing shock with a kiss that told her he was deadly serious.

Micha pulled Maria over him and stared up at his incredible wife. Her capacity to laugh and to love had always inspired him, and he loved her with a fierceness that surprised him even now. He swept back the curtain of curls that had fallen across her face.

'You *are* serious,' she realised with a half smile that distracted him for a moment.

'Absolutely.'

Maria let out an exasperated sigh that kind of surprised him. Of course, this would absolutely be her decision and he would never want her to do something she didn't want to do. But the thing about the love he felt for her and their children, it was exponential. It never ran out. It just kept increasing and it never filled him completely or stopped because there was just more and more space until it filled everything around them. He'd not quite ever imagined it that way, but it was how it worked for him, for her, for their family. The one they had created despite the difficult personalities in the Gallo clan.

After his marriage to Maria and the challenge her father had tried to mount with Gallo Group, he and Antonio had sat down together, without their wives, and talked properly for the first time since he'd been sent to Paris.

He'd realised in the course of that conversation that he hadn't just lost Maria, but he'd also lost Antonio, who had been acting in defence of Maria. Misunderstandings and miscommunications, furthered by Gio's agenda to see the two cousins together, had kept them apart and it had taken a while to get back into the firm friendship they'd once had as youngsters. And Enzo and Erin had soon become part of their group.

'Of course if you don't want to—'

His words stopped when she slapped him a little harder than necessary on the arm.

'What was that for?' he asked, rubbing his arm.

'You are so *impatient*,' she complained.

What? She wasn't making sense.

'You just had to wait a few hours,' she insisted cryptically.

'For what?' he asked confused.

'And then it would have been a surprise.'

'What would have been a surprise, Maria? Honestly, you—'

This time he cut his own words off as he realised that she was grinning and that her eyes were dancing, glittering in the sun light just like the lake behind them.

Goosebumps broke out across his skin as he realised what she was saying.

'You're pregnant,' he said, lurching upwards and taking her with him so that she sat in his lap. 'We're pregnant!' he yelled.

'You're pregnant?' was echoed by several voices at the same time, as children and adults came to join them on the grass.

Everyone was there, the two other families having arrived one after the other.

Ivy and Erin, arm in arm, looked as if they were going to burst with excitement. Enzo and Antonio, each holding more children than probably safe, looked utterly delighted, but Micha had eyes only for his wife.

'You're pregnant,' he whispered, framing her face with his hands, knowing that she was the most precious thing in the world to him in that moment.

'I am.'

'I love you,' he said. 'I always have and I always will. Only you. For the rest of my life.'

'You are my home, Micha Rufina. My home, my heart,

my hope and my soulmate. I will choose you every day, over and over and over again. You will *always* be my choice.'

And Micha knew it as a truth that kept them together through the hard times, the stressful times, the worrying times, but also the best of times. He was her choice, and she was his heart for the rest of their very happy lives.

* * * * *

If you were captivated by Their Boardroom Baby, *then be sure to check out the previous instalments in the* Filthy Rich Italians trilogy, Inconveniently Wed *and* The Rossetti Ring Requirement. *And why not enjoy these other stories by Pippa Roscoe!*

His Jet-Set Nights with the Innocent
In Bed with Her Billionaire Bodyguard
Twin Consequences of That Night
Greek's Temporary "I Do"
Forbidden Until Midnight

Available now!

Get up to 4 Free Books!

**We'll send you 2 free books from each series you try
PLUS a free Mystery Gift.**

Both the **Harlequin Presents** and **Harlequin Medical Romance** series
feature exciting stories of passion and drama.

YES! Please send me 2 FREE novels from Harlequin Presents or Harlequin Medical Romance and my FREE gift (gift is worth about $10 retail). After receiving them, if I don't wish to receive any more books, I can return the shipping statement marked "cancel." If I don't cancel, I will receive 6 brand-new larger-print novels every month and be billed just $7.19 each in the U.S., or $7.99 each in Canada, or 4 brand-new Harlequin Medical Romance Larger-Print books every month and be billed just $7.19 each in the U.S. or $7.99 each in Canada, a savings of 20% off the cover price. It's quite a bargain! Shipping and handling is just 50¢ per book in the U.S. and $1.25 per book in Canada.* I understand that accepting the 2 free books and gift places me under no obligation to buy anything. I can always return a shipment and cancel at any time. The free books and gift are mine to keep no matter what I decide.

Choose one: ☐ **Harlequin Presents Larger-Print** (176/376 BPA G36Y) ☐ **Harlequin Medical Romance** (171/371 BPA G36Y) ☐ **Or Try Both!** (176/376 & 171/371 BPA G36Z)

Name (please print) _____

Address _____ Apt. # _____

City _____ State/Province _____ Zip/Postal Code _____

Email: Please check this box ☐ if you would like to receive newsletters and promotional emails from Harlequin Enterprises ULC and its affiliates. You can unsubscribe anytime.

Mail to the **Harlequin Reader Service:**
IN U.S.A.: P.O. Box 1341, Buffalo, NY 14240-8531
IN CANADA: P.O. Box 603, Fort Erie, Ontario L2A 5X3

Want to explore our other series or interested in ebooks? Visit www.ReaderService.com or call 1-800-873-8635.

---

*Terms and prices subject to change without notice. Prices do not include sales taxes, which will be charged (if applicable) based on your state or country of residence. Canadian residents will be charged applicable taxes. Offer not valid in Quebec. This offer is limited to one order per household. Books received may not be as shown. Not valid for current subscribers to the Harlequin Presents or Harlequin Medical Romance series. All orders subject to approval. Credit or debit balances in a customer's account(s) may be offset by any other outstanding balance owed by or to the customer. Please allow 4 to 6 weeks for delivery. Offer available while quantities last.

Your Privacy—Your information is being collected by Harlequin Enterprises ULC, operating as Harlequin Reader Service. For a complete summary of the information we collect, how we use this information and to whom it is disclosed, please visit our privacy notice located at https://corporate.harlequin.com/privacy-notice. Notice to California Residents – Under California law, you have specific rights to control and access your data. For more information on these rights and how to exercise them, visit https://corporate.harlequin.com/california-privacy. For additional information for residents of other U.S. states that provide their residents with certain rights with respect to personal data, visit https://corporate.harlequin.com/other-state-residents-privacy-rights/.